SHIPS

by

Brian Benson

GROSSET & DUNLAP
A National General Company
Publishers · New York

Managing Editor Peter Usborne
Editors Su Swallow, Susan Ellis, Chris Milsome
Illustrators John Batchelor
          Brian Hiley
          William Hobson
          Frank Friend
          Tony Mitchell
          Jack Pelling
Illustrations consultant John W. Wood
Projects R. H. Warring
Picture Research Marion Gain, Ann Usborne

Published in the United States by
Grosset & Dunlap, Inc.
New York, N.Y.
FIRST PRINTING 1971

contents

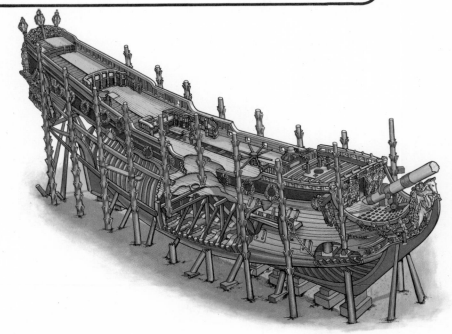

Made and printed by
Litografia A. Romero, S.A.,
Tenerife (Spain)

The first boats

Dug-out canoe 6000 B.C.

Logs and rafts

Man's first attempts to conquer water were, no doubt, by swimming. In one of those early swimming expeditions one man must have grabbed hold of a floating log, and so became the first man to use a boat.

For tens of thousands of years boats were just fallen logs, paddled by hand. One day, someone thought of lashing two logs together to form the first raft.

In another part of the world, another man found that an armful of reeds would keep him afloat.

These discoveries must have been made many times over because in those days people lived in separate little tribes and there was little contact between one tribe and the next.

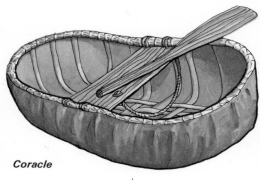

Coracle

Balsa wood raft

Three early boats

Three basic types of boat began to appear all over the world. One was the dug-out canoe. This was a log hollowed out by fire or an axe. This kind of canoe is still used in the islands of the Pacific.

The early rafts were made from balsa wood or reeds. The explorer Thor Heyerdahl copied the early rafts for making the *Kon-tiki* and the *Ra*.

The skin-covered boat probably developed from a bundle of reeds covered by an animal skin to form a float. The coracle and the Eskimo kayak may have come from the early skin covered boats.

One of the first boats (above) was made from a single tree trunk. Variations of this craft can still be found all over the world where there are many trees.

The coracle (left) is made by forming a framework of withes, or reeds. Then skins are stretched over the frame. This kind of boat was used wherever there were no trees suitable for dug-out canoes. Very large ones were sometimes used to carry loads.

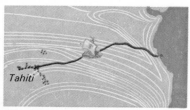

Tahiti

Kon-Tiki route 1950

Norwegian explorer Thor Heyerdahl sailed across the Pacific with a group of explorers in a balsa wood raft (left). The raft was made using primitive methods and materials.

Heyerdahl sailed 4,300 miles in his raft *Kon-Tiki* (above). He wanted to prove that Polynesian aborigines could have sailed from South America in a similar raft 1,500 years ago.

Egyptian papyrus raft

The early Egyptians built rafts from bundles of reeds tied together (left). They used papyrus reeds which grew along the banks of the Nile.

A sailing version of this raft (below) developed as man learned to use the wind. The cabin was probably for an important official.

Egyptian sailing raft

3

War and trade early Mediterranean ships

Egyptian river boat c. 2000 B.C.

A typical Egyptian river boat (above) was found in a tomb. The large oar was for steering.

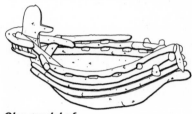

Clay model of Cypriot ship c. 500 B.C.

The model above is of a light cargo ship, as it is very round with high sides. Like contemporary Greek ships, this may have been built of pine, with a spruce mast.

Greek galley c. 500 B.C.

At the battle of Salamis a fleet of about 1,000 Persian ships was defeated by some 300 Greek galleys, or triremes (above). A typical trireme was about 140ft long and 16ft wide.

Roman merchant ship c. 200 A.D.

This merchant ship may have carried corn from Egypt to Rome.

Ship design in Egypt

The primitive boat shapes gradually changed as men discovered small improvements. The early rafts first became saucer-shaped, which helped to keep the crew dry. Then they became longer, which made them easier to steer. Wooden paddles were better than paddling with hands and a much longer paddle was used at the back, or stern, to steer the boat.

Two major changes happened soon after this in Egypt. First a papyrus boat was built with a small square sail. This must have been the first time that man could travel without effort. Then about 2,700 years before the birth of Christ (B.C.), the Egyptians started making ships out of short narrow planks of wood. They used acacia and sycamore, the only trees that grew in the Nile Delta.

The first keel

Soon the Egyptians were sailing all around the eastern Mediterranean. They traded with other countries, and bought much longer planks, hewn from cedar trees in Phoenicia. The early designers could build better ships with these planks.

The giant cedar planks from Phoenicia (now the Lebanon) were long and straight enough to go the whole length of the ship, and these were used as the first keels. The keel is still an important part of a ship, as it strengthens the boat and keeps it from bending in the middle. The long planks also meant that the short paddles could be replaced by longer oars which pivoted on part of the boat. These developments took place about 1500 B.C.

Phoenician warships

The Phoenicians then took the lead from the Egyptians in boat design. The Phoenicians were brave sailors, and sailed all over the Mediterranean. They fought many fierce sea battles with other powerful Mediterranean nations, whose warships were copied from the Phoenician design.

Early trade

The long, narrow Phoenician galleys were not big enough to carry cargoes. Nor could the owners afford the large numbers of men needed to row them. So a shorter, broader ship with one large square sail came into use, and remained the standard Mediterranean cargo ship for many centuries.

The early Mediterranean trade was in luxury goods—wine, honey, oils and ivory. Metal ores were wanted—particularly tin and copper. Rome imported grain from Egypt to feed her people, and wild animals from Africa to entertain them. Rome also imported the treasure stolen from conquered nations.

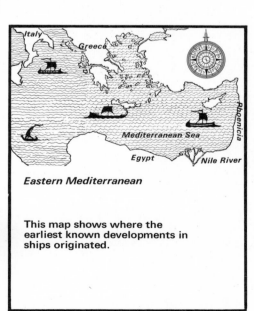

Eastern Mediterranean

This map shows where the earliest known developments in ships originated.

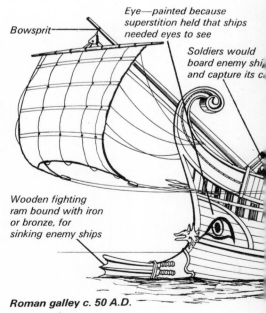

Eye—painted because superstition held that ships needed eyes to see

Bowsprit

Soldiers would board enemy shi and capture its c

Wooden fighting ram bound with iron or bronze, for sinking enemy ships

Roman galley c. 50 A.D.

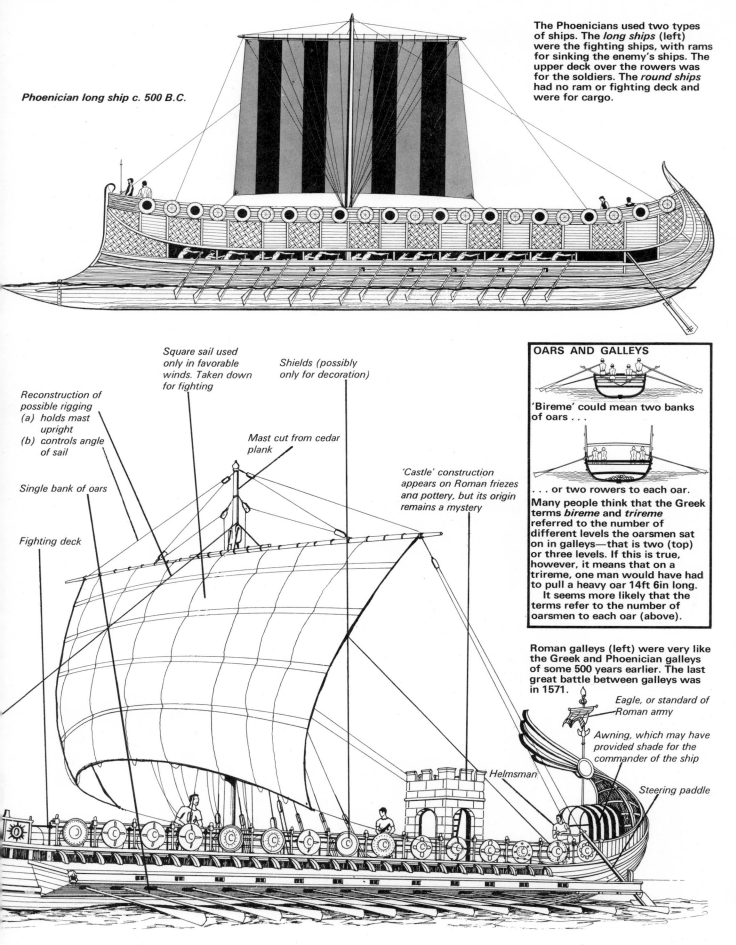

Phoenician long ship c. 500 B.C.

The Phoenicians used two types of ships. The *long ships* (left) were the fighting ships, with rams for sinking the enemy's ships. The upper deck over the rowers was for the soldiers. The *round ships* had no ram or fighting deck and were for cargo.

Square sail used only in favorable winds. Taken down for fighting

Shields (possibly only for decoration)

Reconstruction of possible rigging
(a) holds mast upright
(b) controls angle of sail

Mast cut from cedar plank

Single bank of oars

'Castle' construction appears on Roman friezes and pottery, but its origin remains a mystery

Fighting deck

OARS AND GALLEYS

'Bireme' could mean two banks of oars . . .

. . . or two rowers to each oar.
Many people think that the Greek terms *bireme* and *trireme* referred to the number of different levels the oarsmen sat on in galleys—that is two (top) or three levels. If this is true, however, it means that on a trireme, one man would have had to pull a heavy oar 14ft 6in long.

It seems more likely that the terms refer to the number of oarsmen to each oar (above).

Roman galleys (left) were very like the Greek and Phoenician galleys of some 500 years earlier. The last great battle between galleys was in 1571.

Eagle, or standard of Roman army

Awning, which may have provided shade for the commander of the ship

Helmsman

Steering paddle

5

Ships of the Dark Ages

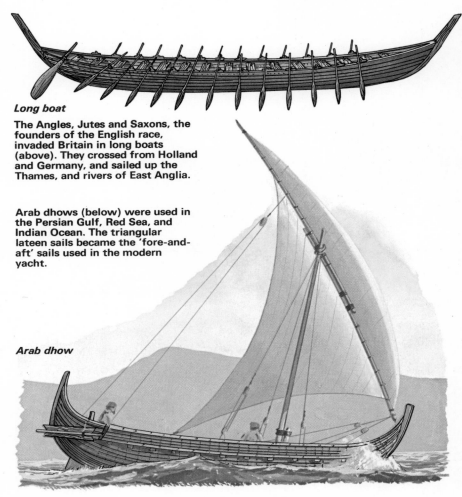

Long boat

The Angles, Jutes and Saxons, the founders of the English race, invaded Britain in long boats (above). They crossed from Holland and Germany, and sailed up the Thames, and rivers of East Anglia.

Arab dhows (below) were used in the Persian Gulf, Red Sea, and Indian Ocean. The triangular lateen sails became the 'fore-and-aft' sails used in the modern yacht.

Arab dhow

Viking merchant ship 7th to 10th century

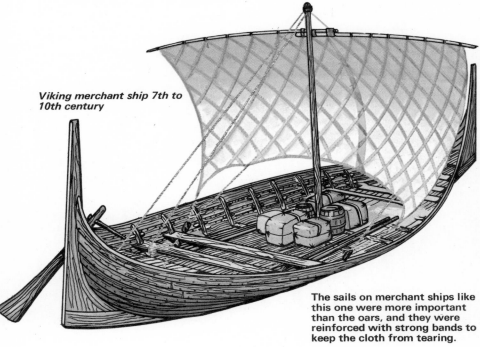

The sails on merchant ships like this one were more important than the oars, and they were reinforced with strong bands to keep the cloth from tearing.

Invasion of Britain

Early developments in ship design came from the Mediterranean area. As the great Roman Empire collapsed, however, the northern European tribes came into their own.

The first major expeditions mounted by the northern Europeans were the raids on Britain. They crossed the English Channel and the North Sea in long open boats.

These long boats developed into the Viking long-ships, which carried the fierce Scandinavian warriors on raids and conquests all over Europe.

King Alfred's dragon boats

The earliest recorded sea battle in these northern waters was between the Scandinavians and the English. King Alfred of England built larger boats than the Viking long ships, called dragon boats. The fleet of dragon boats, which was the beginning of the Royal Navy, fought off the raiders.

The Viking Danes soon copied the dragon boat design. They often sailed to Greenland in their new ships, where they founded a colony. It is even possible that they sailed to North America in them hundreds of years before Columbus.

William the Conqueror's ships were also like King Alfred's dragon boats.

A replica of a Viking ship crossed the Atlantic in 28 days in 1893.

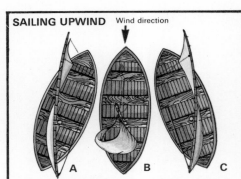

SAILING UPWIND Wind direction

A   B   C

The triangular lateen sails, set almost in line with the length of the ship (therefore, fore-and-aft sails) were the forerunner of almost every kind of modern sail. The wind blows around the sail, which is curved like the upper surface of an aircraft wing. This produces a 'lift' that moves the boat forward. By 'tacking' (zig-zagging either side of the wind direction) a lateen-rigged boat can sail upwind (A and C), although if the boat heads directly into the wind (B) the sail collapses and the boat does not move.

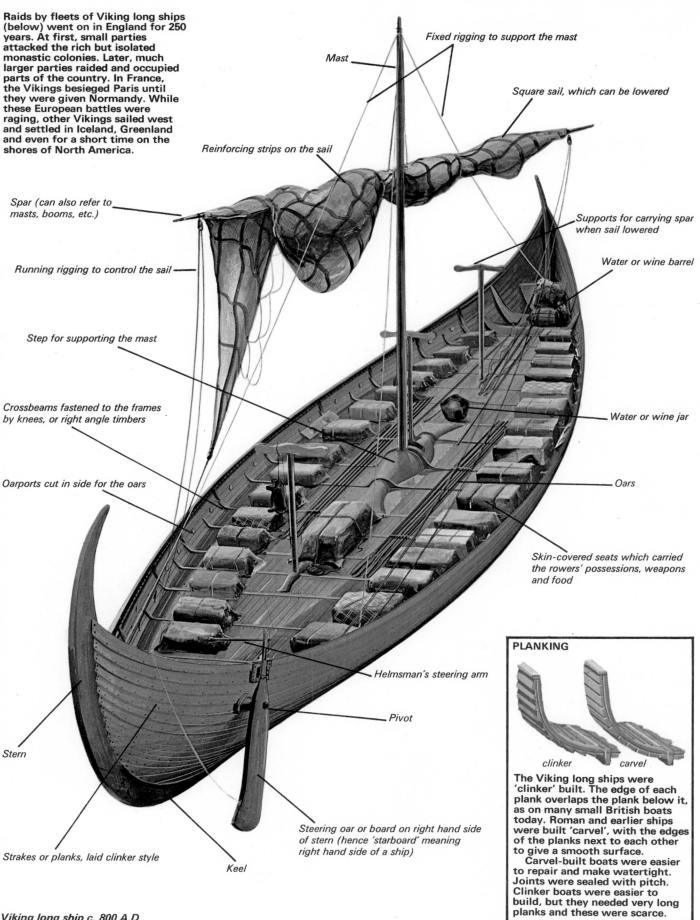

Raids by fleets of Viking long ships (below) went on in England for 250 years. At first, small parties attacked the rich but isolated monastic colonies. Later, much larger parties raided and occupied parts of the country. In France, the Vikings besieged Paris until they were given Normandy. While these European battles were raging, other Vikings sailed west and settled in Iceland, Greenland and even for a short time on the shores of North America.

Mast

Fixed rigging to support the mast

Square sail, which can be lowered

Reinforcing strips on the sail

Spar (can also refer to masts, booms, etc.)

Supports for carrying spar when sail lowered

Water or wine barrel

Running rigging to control the sail

Step for supporting the mast

Water or wine jar

Crossbeams fastened to the frames by knees, or right angle timbers

Oarports cut in side for the oars

Oars

Skin-covered seats which carried the rowers' possessions, weapons and food

Helmsman's steering arm

Pivot

Stern

Steering oar or board on right hand side of stern (hence 'starboard' meaning right hand side of a ship)

Strakes or planks, laid clinker style

Keel

Viking long ship c. 800 A.D.

PLANKING

clinker   *carvel*

The Viking long ships were 'clinker' built. The edge of each plank overlaps the plank below it, as on many small British boats today. Roman and earlier ships were built 'carvel', with the edges of the planks next to each other to give a smooth surface.

Carvel-built boats were easier to repair and make watertight. Joints were sealed with pitch. Clinker boats were easier to build, but they needed very long planks and these were scarce.

The explorers

Cog boat c. 1200 A.D.

The towers at each end of the cog boat (above), like small castles, were to help defend the ship, or to attack another ship. There were no guns in those days. Sea battles were fought with the attacking ship alongside the enemy ship. Then soldiers, hiding in the castles, would try to board the other ship just as if they were storming a land castle.

Christopher Columbus

Columbus (above) persuaded the Queen of Spain to finance an expedition around the world to India. He commanded three small ships. The largest, the *Santa Maria* (right), was a carrack, or *nao*, a common Spanish trading ship with three masts.

Vasco da Gama

Ferdinand Magellan

Vasco da Gama (above left), a Portuguese explorer, was the first known European to visit India by sea. He was as famous in Portugal as Drake became in England.

Another Portuguese adventurer was Ferdinand Magellan (above right). Magellan quareled with the King of Portugal and went to work for Spain.

The next major development in the history of the sea concerned mainly the sailors rather than their ships. The Renaissance period is famous for its art, writing, and its discoveries. It was also the period of great voyages of exploration.

In 1488, Bartholomew Diaz sailed a small ship right down the coast of Africa and around the Cape of Good Hope.

Explorers who sailed to the west included Christopher Columbus, an Italian who worked for the Spaniards. He sailed west to find another route to China and India. Much to his and everyone else's surprise, he found America, although he was probably not the first explorer there. The Viking Danes, and the Ancient Egyptians, probably also discovered the Americas.

Ferdinand Magellan, a Portuguese explorer, sailed around South America and he and his crew became the first western sailors to sail 'round the Horn.' The Magellan Strait, at the tip of South America is named after him.

The ships used by most of these explorers were developed from the dragon boats. By about 1200, however, the English had developed a sailing cargo boat, which was shorter and broader than a dragon boat. These cog boats were used throughout Europe and the Mediterranean. They were very stable and seaworthy.

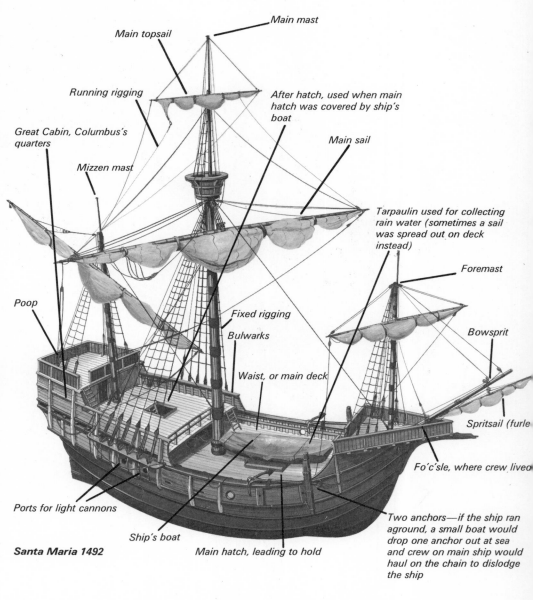

Main topsail — *Main mast*

Running rigging

After hatch, used when main hatch was covered by ship's boat

Great Cabin, Columbus's quarters

Main sail

Mizzen mast

Tarpaulin used for collecting rain water (sometimes a sail was spread out on deck instead)

Foremast

Poop

Fixed rigging

Bulwarks

Bowsprit

Waist, or main deck

Spritsail (furle

Fo'c'sle, where crew lived

Ports for light cannons

Ship's boat

Santa Maria 1492

Main hatch, leading to hold

Two anchors—if the ship ran aground, a small boat would drop one anchor out at sea and crew on main ship would haul on the chain to dislodge the ship

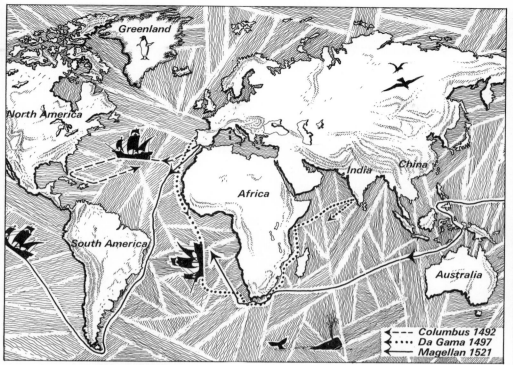

The map (left) shows the new sea routes discovered by the great explorers of the Renaissance period. These men would set out with a fleet of four or five small ships and a crew of about 250. They often had to face a year or two of storms, hostile natives, disease and mutiny before returning home.

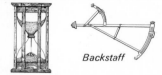

Backstaff

Sand-glass

The backstaff was just one of many instruments of navigation used by the explorers. It was used to find the angle between the sun and the horizon, which, if measured at a specific time, determined the ship's distance from the Equator.

The sand-glass, or hour glass, was used to regulate the ship's watches, and as a clock. Some ran for four hours, others for only one hour.

Greenland

North America

Africa

India

China

South America

Australia

- - - *Columbus 1492*
····· *Da Gama 1497*
——— *Magellan 1521*

New sea routes 1400's and 1500's

A peculiar ship of this time was the caravel (left), mainly used in the Mediterranean. Two of Columbus's ships were caravels. The hull is similar to other hulls of the period, but the rigging is very different.

Lateen sails were carried on all but the foremast, which carried a square sail. But it was soon realized that the conventional rig of square sails on the fore and main masts was more effective.

Caravel 15th century

9

England against Spain guns at sea

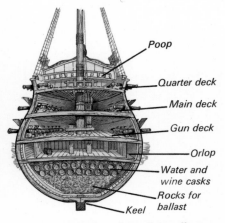

Cross-section of English galleon

The gun deck of the English galleons (above) had to be well above the water line, otherwise water would come through the gunports when the ship heeled over. These ships carried 16 heavy, or culverin cannons and 14 lighter demi-culverin guns.

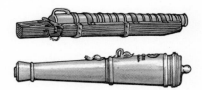

Typical brass guns of the Armada

The battle of the Armada was the first battle fought by gunfire alone, although ships first carried guns about 1350. Cast brass guns (above) were replacing the wrought and cast iron guns. They were cheaper and less dangerous to those firing them.

The fight for new lands

The success of the early Spanish and Portuguese explorers was no great surprise in England. Ships sailing from Spain or Portugal had the advantage of moderate trade winds. Sailors from northern Europe had the fierce North Atlantic to contend with.

Within a few years English, Spanish and Portuguese ships were trading all along the coasts of North and Central America and East Africa. Fights frequently broke out among the sailors, who were all trying to make their fortunes. The religious and political differences between Spain and England during the reign of Queen Elizabeth I meant that a state of war existed at sea during the whole of the second half of the 16th century. War between Spain and Portugal was avoided by Pope Alexander VI who divided the New World between them. Protestant England, of course, did not agree with his division, and many bloody battles followed.

Battle of the Armada

All the fighting and ill will between Spain and England came to a climax in 1588, when a great Spanish fleet sailed to invade England. This fleet of 28 special fighting ships, 40 large merchant ships used as war ships and 55 transports and smaller ships, was broken up by an English fleet of about the same size in the battle of the Armada. For although the two sides had about the same number of ships, the ships were very different. Ships of both countries had built up the aftercastle, or poop, but the English ships had abandoned the forecastle (fo'c'sle). The high sides of the old forecastle had made maneuvering very difficult, since they caught the wind. The English ships were also better shaped under the water. This made the English ships faster.

Cannons

By this time, guns had been in use for over a century. In 1501 a Frenchman, Descharges of Brest, was the first to cut holes in the sides of ships to allow guns to be carried below the top deck.

The Spanish ships carried heavy short-range cannons and demi-cannons, firing heavy cannon balls. The English relied on lighter ones. The Spanish tried to grapple an enemy so that their soldiers could board the enemy ships. The English kept out of range of the Spanish, but caused a lot of damage with long range guns.

A medium-sized English galleon (right) measured about 150ft long and 38ft broad, with a crew of 500. Heavy stones, the stores and water barrels were kept in the hold to keep the ship upright.

HAND WEAPONS

1 Pistol; 2 Powder pouch; 3 Musket; 4 Pike; 5 Cutlass; 6 Scabbard (sheath); 7 Dirk (dagger)

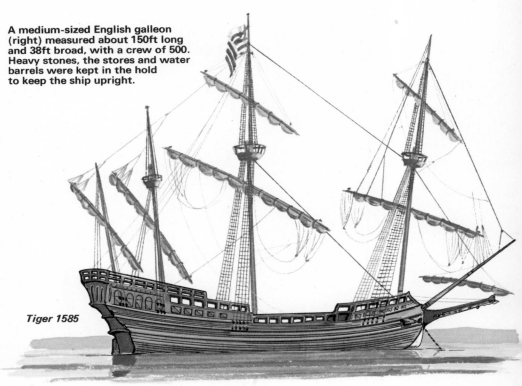

Tiger 1585

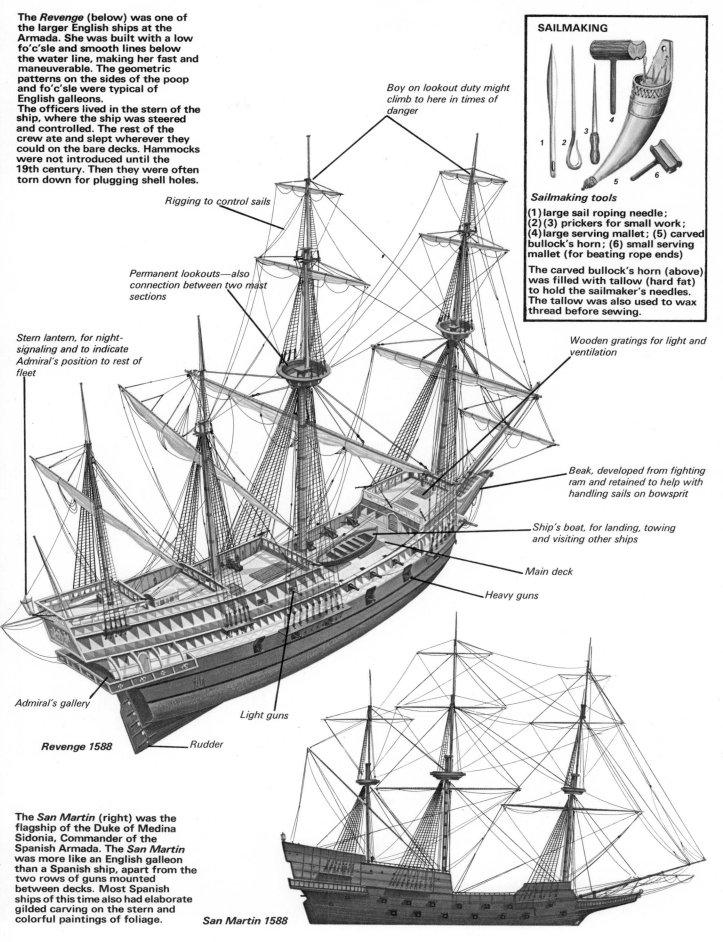

The *Revenge* (below) was one of the larger English ships at the Armada. She was built with a low fo'c'sle and smooth lines below the water line, making her fast and maneuverable. The geometric patterns on the sides of the poop and fo'c'sle were typical of English galleons.
The officers lived in the stern of the ship, where the ship was steered and controlled. The rest of the crew ate and slept wherever they could on the bare decks. Hammocks were not introduced until the 19th century. Then they were often torn down for plugging shell holes.

Boy on lookout duty might climb to here in times of danger

Rigging to control sails

Permanent lookouts—also connection between two mast sections

Stern lantern, for night-signaling and to indicate Admiral's position to rest of fleet

Wooden gratings for light and ventilation

Beak, developed from fighting ram and retained to help with handling sails on bowsprit

Ship's boat, for landing, towing and visiting other ships

Main deck

Heavy guns

Admiral's gallery

Light guns

Revenge 1588

Rudder

SAILMAKING

Sailmaking tools

(1) large sail roping needle;
(2) (3) prickers for small work;
(4) large serving mallet; (5) carved bullock's horn; (6) small serving mallet (for beating rope ends)

The carved bullock's horn (above) was filled with tallow (hard fat) to hold the sailmaker's needles. The tallow was also used to wax thread before sewing.

The *San Martin* (right) was the flagship of the Duke of Medina Sidonia, Commander of the Spanish Armada. The *San Martin* was more like an English galleon than a Spanish ship, apart from the two rows of guns mounted between decks. Most Spanish ships of this time also had elaborate gilded carving on the stern and colorful paintings of foliage.

San Martin 1588

The settlements of America

Spanish great ship 1500's

The great ship (above), with its high poop and fo'c'sle was used by the early Spanish colonists. It remained in use in Spain for many years. It is typical of the Spanish ships in the battle of the Armada.

The first settlements

The first known successful settlements in the New World were Spanish. Large Spanish colonies were established in the Caribbean, or Spanish Main, and on the mainland of Central and South America, and in Florida. The early Spanish settlers were attracted by all the treasure to be found there. These settlements were raided and plundered by Drake in Elizabeth I's reign.

At the same time, the English picked up the old idea of the Vikings, who had tried to settle on what is thought was the Cape of Newfoundland.

The Pilgrim Fathers

Apart from the adventurous and the unemployed, there was a new group who became the most celebrated settlers in North America. These were the Pilgrims. They were Puritans who had to leave England because of religious persecution. They had left England to settle in Holland, but after ten unhappy years, they decided to try the New World. They finally sailed in 1620, on board the *Mayflower*.

Meanwhile, the Dutch had settled in New York, and the French along the St. Lawrence River in Canada.

FOUNDING OF THE HUDSON'S BAY COMPANY

Nonsuch's route 1668

By 1650, when the *Nonsuch* was built, the French settlers in Canada had built up a profitable trade in beaver furs. But the furs had to be brought from the Hudson Bay area in the north by a laborious inland water route to the St. Lawrence.

In 1668 the *Nonsuch* became the first ship to sail directly into Hudson Bay. The furs could now be shipped directly to Europe. A replica of the *Nonsuch* (below) commemorates the founding of the Hudson's Bay Company, the result of the tiny ship's successful voyage.

Replica of Nonsuch

Indian canoe

The early explorers in North America found that the Indians used canoes (above) made with skin and bark stretched over a frame. The explorers soon adopted these boats themselves because they were light enough to carry around rapids and waterfalls.

12

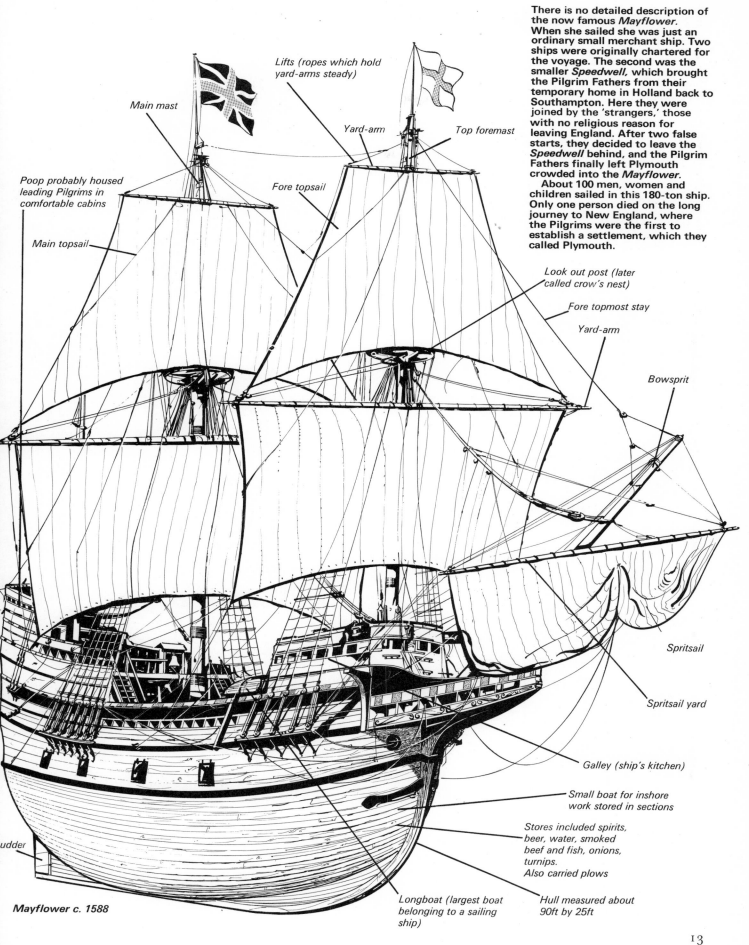

Main mast

Lifts (ropes which hold
yard-arms steady)

Yard-arm

Top foremast

There is no detailed description of
the now famous *Mayflower.*
When she sailed she was just an
ordinary small merchant ship. Two
ships were originally chartered for
the voyage. The second was the
smaller *Speedwell,* which brought
the Pilgrim Fathers from their
temporary home in Holland back to
Southampton. Here they were
joined by the 'strangers,' those
with no religious reason for
leaving England. After two false
starts, they decided to leave the
Speedwell behind, and the Pilgrim
Fathers finally left Plymouth
crowded into the *Mayflower.*

About 100 men, women and
children sailed in this 180-ton ship.
Only one person died on the long
journey to New England, where
the Pilgrims were the first to
establish a settlement, which they
called Plymouth.

Poop probably housed
leading Pilgrims in
comfortable cabins

Fore topsail

Main topsail

Look out post (later
called crow's nest)

Fore topmost stay

Yard-arm

Bowsprit

Spritsail

Spritsail yard

Galley (ship's kitchen)

Small boat for inshore
work stored in sections

Stores included spirits,
beer, water, smoked
beef and fish, onions,
turnips.
Also carried plows

Rudder

Mayflower c. 1588

Longboat (largest boat
belonging to a sailing
ship)

Hull measured about
90ft by 25ft

Shipbuilding in the 17th century

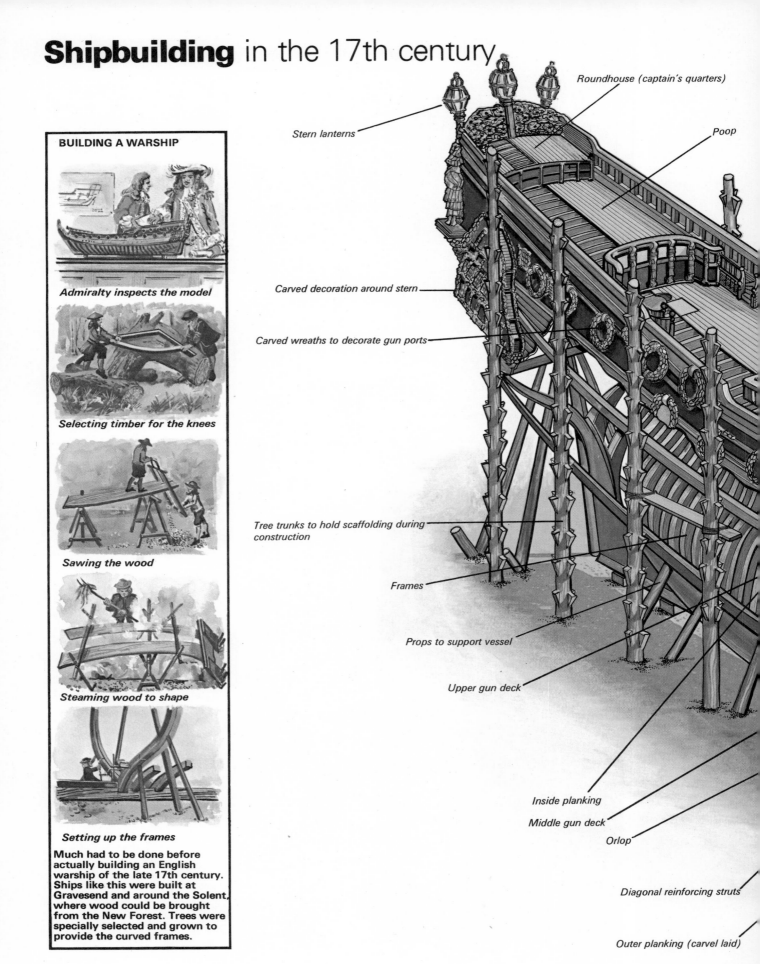

BUILDING A WARSHIP

Admiralty inspects the model

Selecting timber for the knees

Sawing the wood

Steaming wood to shape

Setting up the frames

Much had to be done before actually building an English warship of the late 17th century. Ships like this were built at Gravesend and around the Solent, where wood could be brought from the New Forest. Trees were specially selected and grown to provide the curved frames.

Stern lanterns

Roundhouse (captain's quarters)

Poop

Carved decoration around stern

Carved wreaths to decorate gun ports

Tree trunks to hold scaffolding during construction

Frames

Props to support vessel

Upper gun deck

Inside planking

Middle gun deck

Orlop

Diagonal reinforcing struts

Outer planking (carvel laid)

Design and decoration

European warship design followed the pattern of the galleon for 300 years. The sails and hull shape were basically the same, although they became larger and stronger.

Ships were now designed by first drawing the proposed ship in detail. Then a model was made, which could be studied before the ship was built.

The hull was made much stronger by using reinforcing struts across the width of the ship, and timber was being specially grown with natural curves for the frames, although steaming was necessary to get exactly the right shape.

The bows and sterns were decorated with elaborately carved and gilded motifs and figureheads.

The naval powers in Europe had drawn different conclusions from the Armada. The British Admiralty were dismayed at the failure of long-range guns to sink the enemy. They returned to heavy short-range guns to batter the hulls of enemy ships. France on the other hand, relied on light long-range guns to fire at the enemy's masts and rigging.

SHIPWRIGHT'S TOOLS

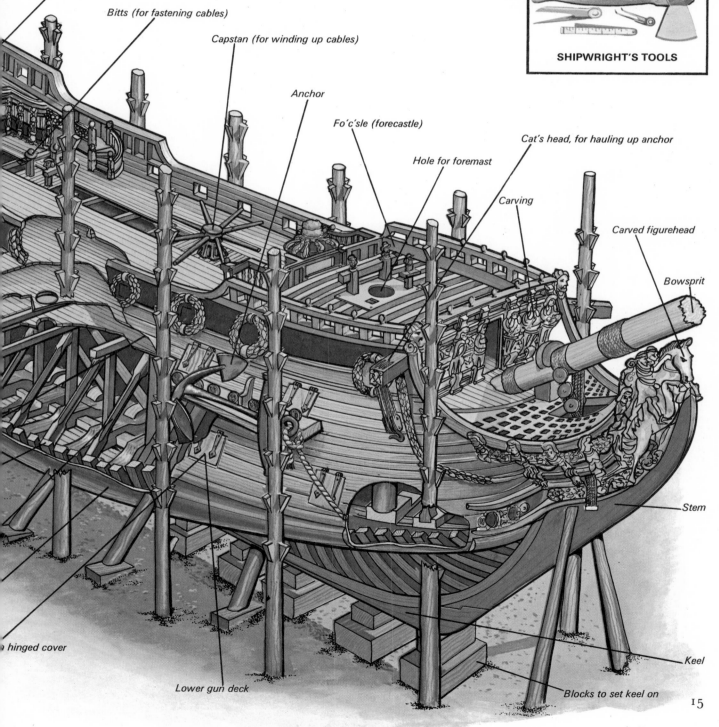

Quarter deck

Bitts (for fastening cables)

Capstan (for winding up cables)

Anchor

Fo'c'sle (forecastle)

Hole for foremast

Cat's head, for hauling up anchor

Carving

Carved figurehead

Bowspit

Stem

Keel

Blocks to set keel on

Lower gun deck

hinged cover

Cargo ships 1600–1800

The map (right) shows the main trade routes of the cargo ships. The slave traders sailed first to the Guinea coast with cheap goods, then to the Caribbean with slaves, and then home again with tobacco or molasses to start again. The *Indiamen* followed the same route at first, but continued southward around South Africa, and eastward to India, Indonesia and China.

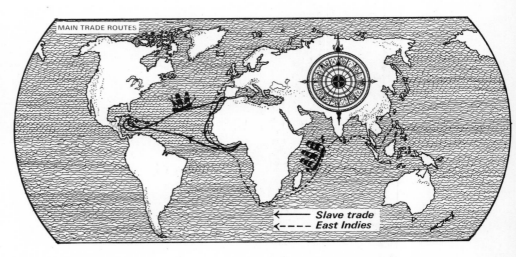

MAIN TRADE ROUTES

⟵ Slave trade
⟵---- East Indies

Typical cargoes
Typical cargoes (above) were timber and tar from Sweden, bales of wool from England, slaves from Africa and tea from China.

Although the spices and slave trades were the most glamorous trades of the time, most of the goods carried to Europe were carried in solid merchant ships like the cat bark (right). It was developed from the cog boats of two centuries earlier.

Similar ships took the whale hunters to the Arctic, and were chosen by Captain Cook for his voyages in the Pacific, when he discovered Australia. Seafaring in northern waters had now become so peaceful that these ships were not fitted for guns.

The Thames barge (far right) was used mainly for carrying cargoes in the Thames Estuary, and also for unloading big ships.

The lee boards on the lee side, or the side away from the wind, could be lowered and acted as a keel.

Trading companies

Groups of merchants formed companies which had sole rights to trade with certain areas of the world. The best known of these was the British East India Company. The history of this company is also the history of British rule in India until the 19th century, for it was the company that raised armies and launched fleets.

The main trade in the 17th century was spices, coming mainly from the East Indies. By 1670 the East India Company was also trading with Formosa and Japan. In the early years, the Company's annual exports were worth about $100,000. By 1675, exports had grown to about one million and imports were about two million. Special ships called *East Indiamen* were built for this trading. The voyages were timed to take advantage of the Trade Winds in the South Atlantic, and the Monsoons in the Indian Ocean.

The slave trade

The other trade to grow in this period was the slave trade. Ships sailed from Europe and America carrying cheap, bright goods to the coast of Guinea. There they traded these goods to local Africans in exchange for African slaves captured from the interior. As many as 700 slaves were often crowded into one small ship. They were carried to the West Indies, or the southern parts of the U.S. and sold to work on sugar, tobacco and, later, cotton plantations. The ships, cleaned, would then return home with a cargo of tobacco or molasses.

Cat bark

Thames barge 1760

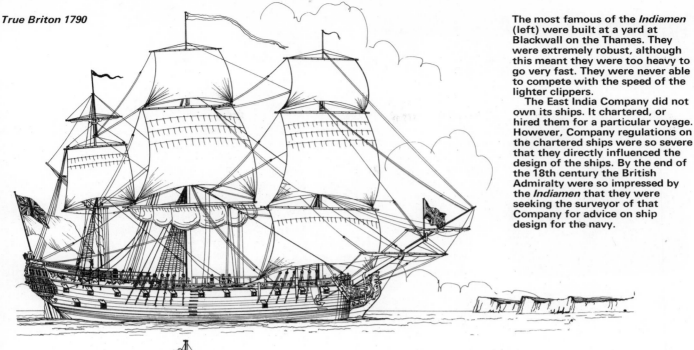

True Briton 1790

The most famous of the *Indiamen* (left) were built at a yard at Blackwall on the Thames. They were extremely robust, although this meant they were too heavy to go very fast. They were never able to compete with the speed of the lighter clippers.

The East India Company did not own its ships. It chartered, or hired them for a particular voyage. However, Company regulations on the chartered ships were so severe that they directly influenced the design of the ships. By the end of the 18th century the British Admiralty were so impressed by the *Indiamen* that they were seeking the surveyor of that Company for advice on ship design for the navy.

Herring Buss 1768

Ships had now been developed for fishing well off the coasts. Other, fast ships were also used to take the catches from the fishing fleets at sea to the markets. The *Herring Buss* (left) was used for catching herring in the North Sea, and north of Scotland. The strange rig developed from the need for a clear deck area to handle the fishing nets.

From fish to furs

The spice and slave trades were the most exciting and valuable carried out at this time. They are also important because they marked the start of world-wide trading. Most of the ships in a European port, however, were 'short trade' ships, carrying a wide range of cargoes over short distances. The cargoes might be anything from woolen goods and turpentine, to timber and supplies of rope (cordage) from the Baltic. Timber and fish came from Newfoundland, a few furs came from Russia and fast little ships brought oranges from Spain and the Portuguese islands of the Azores.

Coasting ships carried coal, stone and salted herring. The sea was the highway of the day, for there were no modern road systems, and no railroads. Inland traffic was carried on rivers, and canals were just being introduced.

The ships of this period, especially those built to the East India Company's requirements, were fairly fast and very robust. The Indiamen and slave ships still carried guns against pirates.

Whaling

A specialist trade of the 18th century was whaling, off the coast of Greenland. This trade was dominated by the Dutch. The whales were harpooned from small rowing boats. The whales were processed at sea, and the whalers, which carried between six and eight rowing boats, brought home only the blubber (for making oil) and whale bone (used to stiffen ladies' dresses).

WHALING OFF GREENLAND

When a whale was sighted it was chased by small boats lowered from the main ship. Crews of four or five men rowed after the whale until they were near enough to harpoon it. If the whale was not killed outright, its struggles could overturn the boat. The men rarely survived in the icy water.

Nelson and Napoleon

Nelson   Napoleon

Napoleon might have conquered Europe but for Nelson's sea power. Napoleon's naval forces never even won a major victory, and were thwarted by the British Royal Navy. Napoleon was finally taken to exile by a ship of the Royal Navy.

Nelson's quarters on the Victory

Even the Admiral's quarters were not luxurious, and he might have to spend up to eight months on board at a time.

Lady Hamilton embroidered the cover on Nelson's day bed, which could be removed to leave the room clear for fighting during a battle.

Nelson's *Agamemnon* (right), a 64 gun ship built in 1781, was a typical third rate ship of the period. The largest share of fighting was done by this class of ship, which carried between 60 and 84 guns.

The *Agamemnon* carried her guns on two decks, with 24 pounders on the lower and 12 pounders on the upper deck. She carried a crew of about 600, including a small force of marines. These sea-going soldiers were to provide landing parties, and to protect the ships' officers from mutinies.

Nelson commanded the *Agamemnon* in the Mediterranean. This ship also served in Nelson's fleets at Copenhagen and Trafalgar.

The Napoleonic Wars

The 18th century was full of wars, particularly the Napoleonic wars between England and France. The short periods of peace simply gave the two countries time to build new weapons. These long and bloody struggles, which made full use of sea power, were headed by the world-famous commanders, Admiral Nelson and Napoleon.

Nelson started his career as a 13-year-old midshipman. He commanded his first ship, a tiny schooner, at only 20. By 25, he was captain of the *Agamemnon*, a fast 64 gun ship-of-the-line.

Nelson's victories

Nelson's victories altered history. The defeat of the French at the Battle of the Nile was the first defeat Napoleonic France had suffered. The French Army, which had planned to conquer Egypt and go towards India, was stranded.

The Battle of Copenhagen persuaded the Danes not to actively aid France in trying to control the Baltic, and may have helped to persuade the Swedes and Russians to desert Napoleon. The final victory, Trafalgar, where Nelson was fatally wounded, was the end of French attempts to dominate the seas.

Agamemnon 1781

Redoubtable

HMS Euryalus

The *Redoubtable* (far left), under the command of Villeneuve, was the flagship of the French fleet at Trafalgar. A musket-ball fired from her mizzen top fatally wounded Nelson, on board the *Victory*.

HMS *Euryalus* (left), a 36-gun frigate, was the first ship of Nelson's fleet to sight the enemy.

Frigates like the *Euryalus* were used to scout for the main fleet, to carry messages, and to attack enemy trade routes. But they were not heavy enough to fight in the 'line of battle', and were not classed as 'ships-of-the-line.' (Until Nelson's time, enemy fleets would run in two close parallel lines to shoot broadside. Ships taking part were known as ships-of-the-line.)

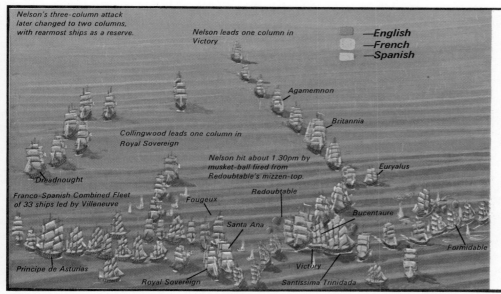

Nelson's three-column attack later changed to two columns, with rearmost ships as a reserve.

Nelson leads one column in *Victory*

— **English**
— **French**
— **Spanish**

Agamemnon

Britannia

Collingwood leads one column in *Royal Sovereign*

Euryalus

Dreadnought

Nelson hit about 1.30pm by musket-ball fired from Redoubtable's mizzen-top.

Franco-Spanish Combined Fleet of 33 ships led by Villeneuve

Redoubtable

Fougeux

Bucentaure

Santa Ana

Formidable

Principe de Asturias

Victory

Royal Sovereign

Santissima Trinidada

BATTLE OF TRAFALGAR 1805

Nelson's method of fighting at sea did not follow the standard pattern. It was usual at that time for two fleets to sail in line alongside each other, and to pound each other to pieces. Nelson, however, attacked at right angles to the enemy fleet and broke through the line to split the enemy fleet up. He then relied on each of his ships to tackle a chosen enemy ship.

On October 21, 1805 Nelson joined battle with the Franco-Spanish combined Fleet off Cape Trafalgar at Cadiz, in Southern Spain. By the end of the day his ships had sunk or captured 22 out of 33 enemy ships, although the English Fleet of 27 ships suffered heavy losses.

Nelson was fatally wounded during his victorious battle, and died later that day on board the *Victory*.

Gundeck

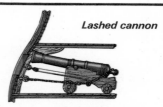

Lashed cannon

The cast iron smooth-bore cannon (above) was still the main armament in Nelson's day. The cannons were lashed down with rope to keep them from rolling.

In battle it was too dangerous to keep too much gunpowder near the guns. So it was kept in the *magazine* room in the middle of the ship, below the water level. Young boys, known as powder monkeys (left), carried the gunpowder to the gundeck as it was needed.

The guns were mounted on both sides of the deck. A crew of five or six handled two opposite guns.

Early steamships

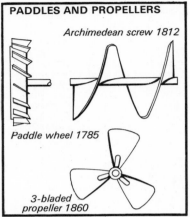
THE COMET ENGINE

This 4hp engine powered the *Comet,* the first steamboat in Europe to run a regular service. She ran for eight years on the Clyde River, in Scotland. The boat was a technical, but not a commercial success.

The steam engine

The first practical steam boat is said to have been *Charlotte Dundas.* She was quickly followed by others, chiefly in Britain and the U.S. The U.S. concentrated mainly on river vessels.

The early steamships were often still built as sailing ships with an engine for entering and leaving harbors, and for use in times of calm.

The *Charlotte Dundas* (below) was built in 1801 by a Scot and is thought to be the first practical steamboat. She was built for Lord Dundas, a wealthy landowner, and named for his wife.

The *Dundas* was designed to replace the horses which towed barges on the Forth and Clyde Canal. Unfortunately the owners of the canal were worried that the wash from the paddle wheel would damage the sides of the canal, and refused to allow her to be used regularly.

Most of these early ships were paddle steamers, but in 1816 an Englishman built a small boat with a propeller. A great argument went on between supporters of paddles and those who favored propellers, but in 1845 it was settled by a contest between two almost identical British war ships. The propeller-driven sloop *Rattler* won all the races against the paddle sloop *Alecto.*

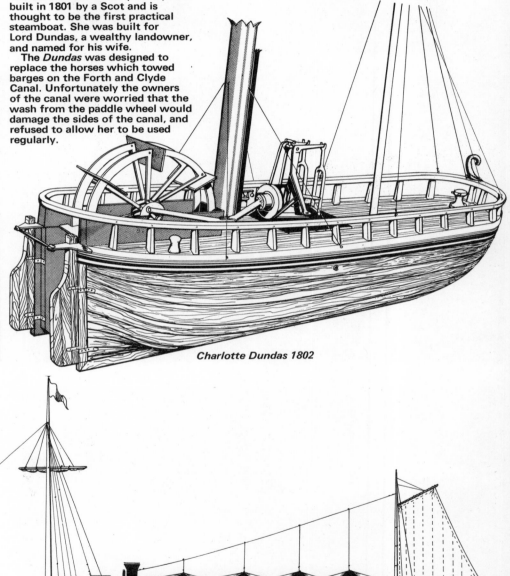

Charlotte Dundas 1802

The *Clermont* (right) was built by an American, Robert Fulton, in 1807. She sailed along the Hudson River, from New York to Albany, covering the 150 miles in 32 hours.

Fulton also built USS *Demologas,* the world's first steam warship.

Clermont 1807

The *Savannah* (left) was the first
steamship to cross the Atlantic, in
1819. She did the voyage in a
record 28 days 11 hours, yet she
only used her engines for 85 hours.
  She was never built with the
idea of crossing the Atlantic. She
was intended for trading between
Savannah and New York. Then the
owners decided that they could sell
her at a profit in Europe, and sent
her there to be sold. But nobody
wanted to buy her and she
eventually sailed back to America.

Savannah 1819

The *Great Britain* was designed by
the great engineer, Isambard
Kingdom Brunel. She was the first
large iron-built, propeller-driven
ship to be used on the Atlantic.
She carried 360 passengers.
After many years' service she was
thought to have ended her days as
a hulk in the Falkland Islands
between South America and the
South Pole. Then in 1970 she was
towed half way around the world to
Bristol, England, to become a
museum.

Great Britain 1843

The *Adriatic* was the last Atlantic
liner built of wood with paddle
wheels. She was not very
successful, and she changed hands
a number of times before she was
finally converted into a sailing ship.

Adriatic 1856

Clippers

Rainbow 1845

The first clipper (above) was designed by an American marine architect, who persuaded some wealthy businessmen to back him.

The *Rainbow's* first trip, in 1845, was not a success—the crew were not used to handling her. The second trip was more profitable, but by 1847 her career was over. On a trip from New York to Peru, she foundered off Cape Horn.

The problems of steam

Not everyone was convinced that the steamship could replace the sailing ship. Steamships needed vast amounts of coal, and special bunkering stations had to be built at the main ports. In countries where coal was not mined, the transport and storage of stocks of coal was expensive. Moreover, those who supported the sailing ship had an even stronger argument when the *clippers,* the most efficient sailing ships ever built, began to appear.

The gold rush

Clippers first made their name carrying passengers to the Californian gold rush at phenomenal speeds. They then came to dominate the transatlantic passenger service, and the immigrant route to Australia. The clippers would sail from California or Australia to China to load tea for America and England.

Then as cheap coal and oil became readily available and engines became more reliable, the clippers lost favor.

One of the most famous clippers was the *Cutty Sark* (right). Today she is preserved at Greenwich, in London. She was built at Aberdeen in Scotland, in 1868, the year before the Suez Canal was opened. She first carried tea from China, and often got home 10 days before her rivals. This meant her tea could be sold for less.

Later the *Cutty Sark* entered the Australian wool trade, and really came into her own as the fastest clipper. In 1887-8 she came home in only 69 days, when the average voyage took 100 days. The saving in time saved money: the upkeep of the crew cost less.

These record speeds and economies were important at a time when sailing ships were fighting for their existence.

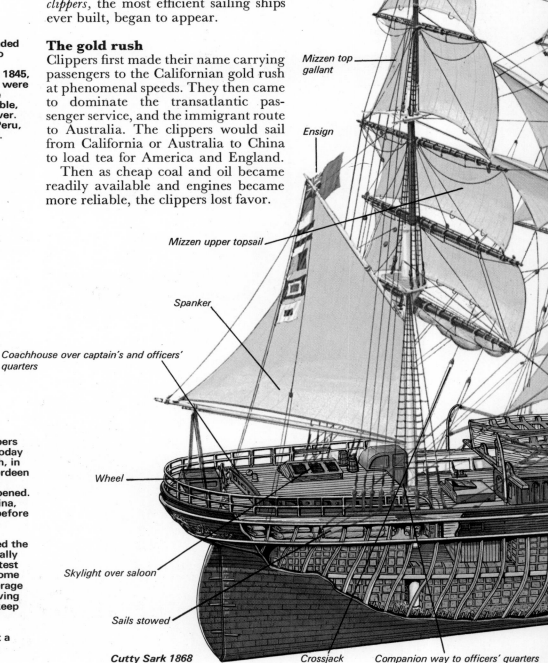

Mizzen mast

Mizzen royal

Mizzen top gallant

Ensign

Mizzen upper topsail

Spanker

Coachhouse over captain's and officers' quarters

Wheel

Skylight over saloon

Sails stowed

Cutty Sark 1868

Crossjack

Companion way to officers' quarters

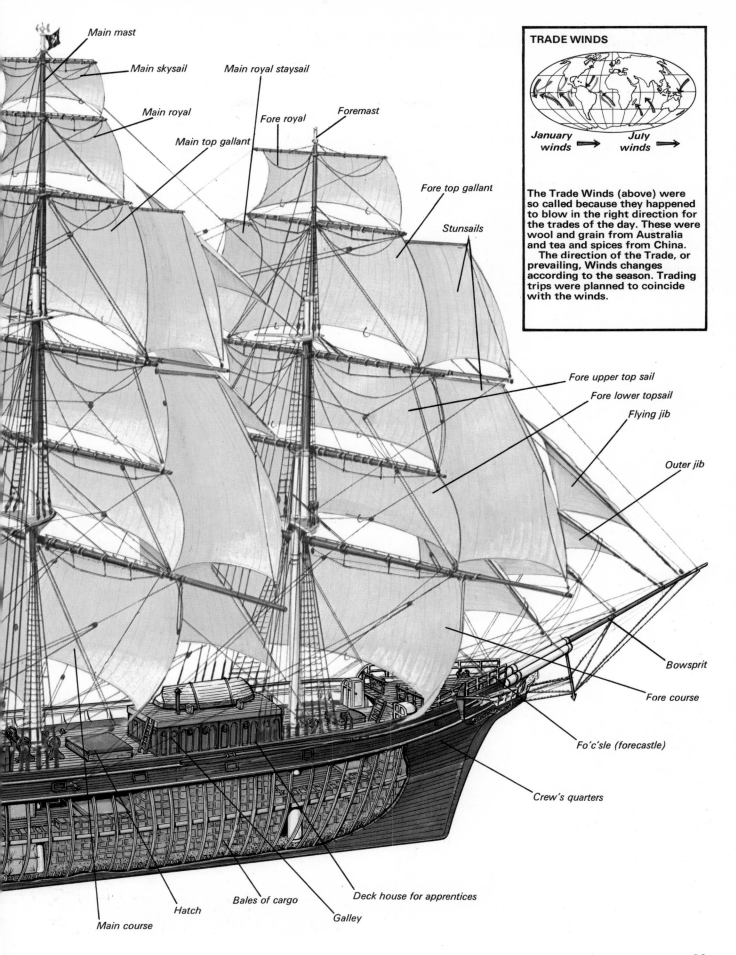

Main mast

Main skysail

Main royal staysail

Main royal

Fore royal

Foremast

Main top gallant

Fore top gallant

Stunsails

Fore upper top sail

Fore lower topsail

Flying jib

Outer jib

Bowsprit

Fore course

Fo´c´sle (forecastle)

Crew's quarters

Deck house for apprentices

Galley

Bales of cargo

Hatch

Main course

23

Triumph of the powered ship

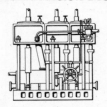

In early engines, steam from the boilers was only used once. In the triple expansion engine (above) the steam is used three times over in three different cylinders. This made the engine cheap to run. It was also reliable and easy to maintain.

The Suez Canal

In 1869 the Suez Canal was opened. It linked the Mediterranean with the Red Sea, and this route saved weeks on a voyage to the East. But the clippers had to be towed through the canal. The close waters of the Mediterranean or the Red Sea did not suit them either.

Soon all the Indian and Chinese trade was taken by steamships, and the clippers left these seas to seek other cargoes. The long haul to Australia was still ideal for them, as steamers would ·have had to stop for coaling, while the sailing ships went through non-stop.

World trade

At the height of the Industrial Revolution, British and German factories were producing the goods sought by the rest of the world. The cargoes included textiles and heavy machinery, such as railroad engines and rails. Coal and oil were also needed. Steam took over on these short haul and heavy traffic routes.

In the 1860's the American Civil War put a stop to England's supply of cotton. So it was brought from India instead. Until the Suez Canal was opened, this meant a long and expensive trip around Africa.

·The *Iberia* is a typical tramp steamer of the 1880's. She was built to carry any type of cargo and would sail from port to port, finding her cargoes as she went. Liners, on the other hand, sailed on set routes or lines, sailing on advertised days, whether they were full or not.

Before steamships could succeed on this type of unscheduled trading, coaling stations had to be set up all over the world, and the engines had to be much more reliable. The *Iberia,* in common with other tramp steamers of her time, kept some rigging, but it was obviously intended only for emergency use. Her main source of power was steam.

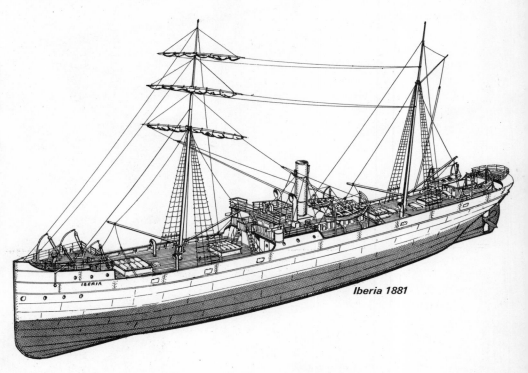

Iberia 1881

The tremendous increase in world trade at the end of the 19th century led to the building of new ships for special cargoes. The most significant of these was the tanker. The *Glückauf* (right) (2,300 tons) is the true prototype of the giant 250,000 ton tankers of today. It was ordered in 1893 by a German company, and built in a Scottish shipyard.

For over a century whale oil had been carried in barrels. When oil was discovered in America larger tanks were carried by sailing ships. In the 1870's steamships were built in England and Sweden with special tanks. Then came the *Glückauf,* the first real tanker.

Glückauf 1893

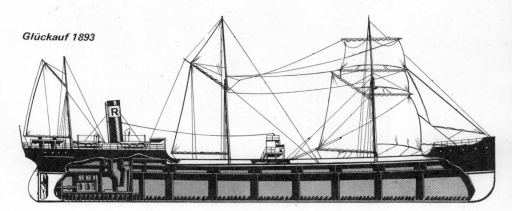

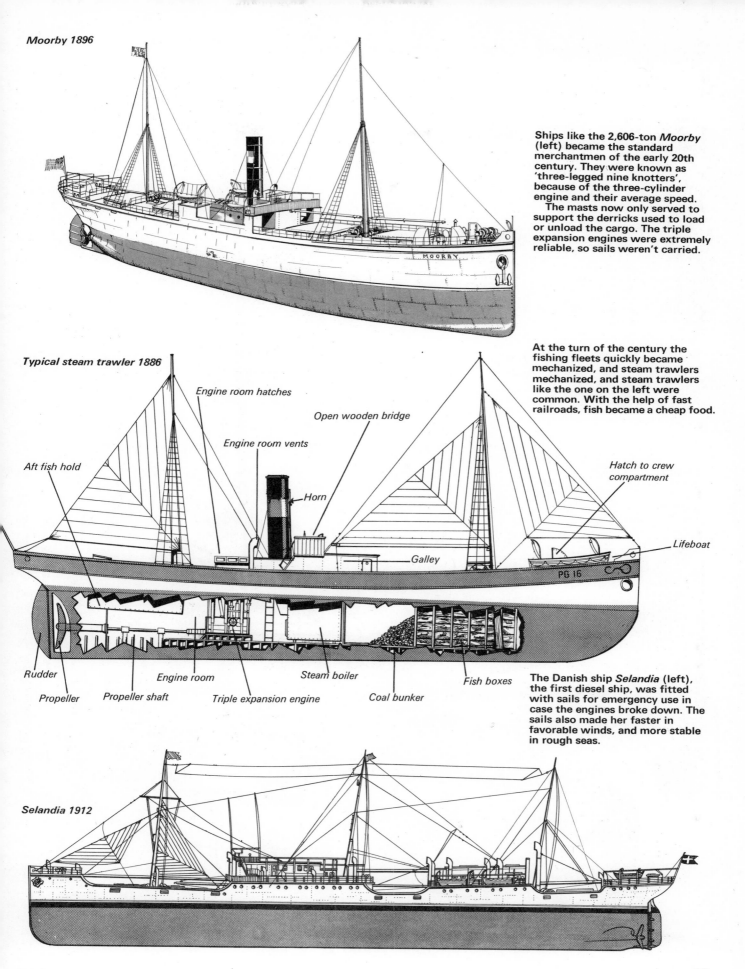

Moorby 1896

Ships like the 2,606-ton *Moorby* (left) became the standard merchantmen of the early 20th century. They were known as 'three-legged nine knotters', because of the three-cylinder engine and their average speed.

The masts now only served to support the derricks used to load or unload the cargo. The triple expansion engines were extremely reliable, so sails weren't carried.

Typical steam trawler 1886

Engine room hatches

Open wooden bridge

Engine room vents

Aft fish hold

Horn

Hatch to crew compartment

Galley

Lifeboat

PG 16

At the turn of the century the fishing fleets quickly became mechanized, and steam trawlers mechanized, and steam trawlers like the one on the left were common. With the help of fast railroads, fish became a cheap food.

Rudder

Propeller

Propeller shaft

Engine room

Triple expansion engine

Steam boiler

Coal bunker

Fish boxes

The Danish ship *Selandia* (left), the first diesel ship, was fitted with sails for emergency use in case the engines broke down. The sails also made her faster in favorable winds, and more stable in rough seas.

Selandia 1912

25

World War I age of the Dreadnought

SMS *Rheinland* (right), one of the Westfalen class of battleships, was Germany's answer to HMS *Dreadnought*. The *Rheinland* carried twelve 11in guns, twelve 5.9in and sixteen 3.4in. She had 11½in armor, displaced 18,900 tons and had a speed of 20 knots.

Dreadnought, on the other hand, carried ten 12in guns and twenty-four 3in guns. Her armor was 11in thick, displacement 17,900 tons and speed 21 knots.

Massive fleets of these battleships threatened each other throughout the four long years of World War I, but the only major battle, that of Jutland in 1916, ended inconclusively.

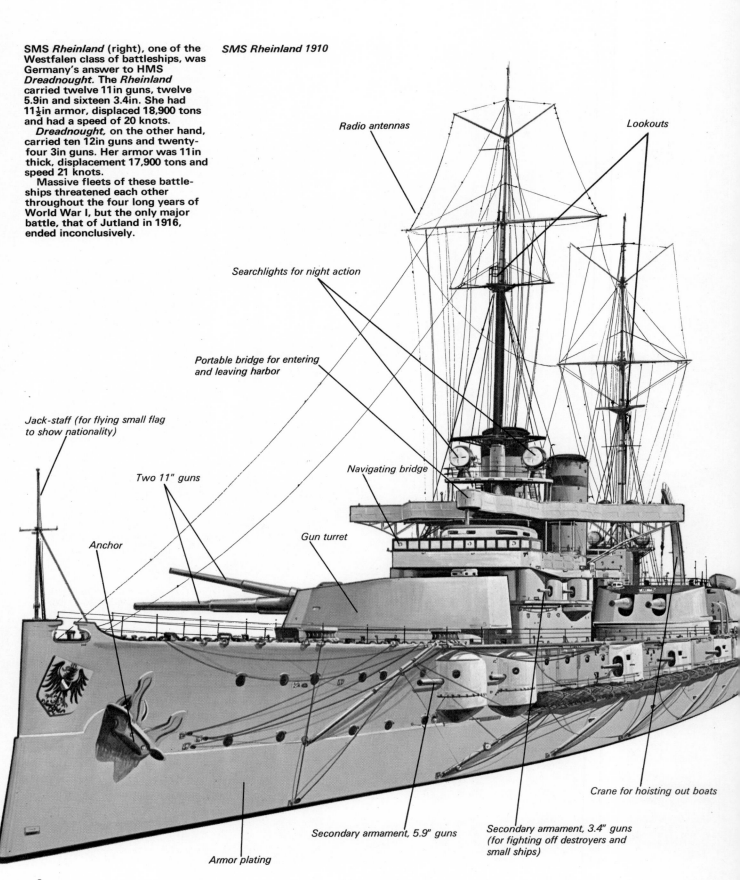

SMS Rheinland 1910

Radio antennas

Lookouts

Searchlights for night action

Portable bridge for entering and leaving harbor

Jack-staff (for flying small flag to show nationality)

Two 11" guns

Navigating bridge

Anchor

Gun turret

Crane for hoisting out boats

Secondary armament, 5.9" guns

Secondary armament, 3.4" guns (for fighting off destroyers and small ships)

Armor plating

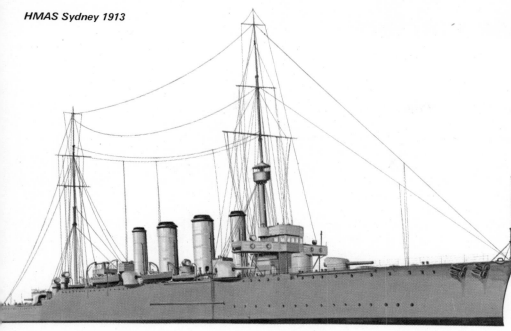

HMAS Sydney 1913

The Australian cruiser HMAS *Sydney* (left), of 5,600 tons, carrying eight 6in guns, was capable of 26 knots. She was to end the success story of the German cruiser SMS *Emden*. The *Sydney* was given a radio warning of *Emden's* plan to cut the telegraph cable between Australia, South Africa and India, on one of the Cocos Islands. To make matters worse, the German lookout misidentified the *Sydney* as a supply ship—a search at sea depended on lookouts on the masts before radar or aircraft were available. When the mistake was realized, *Emden* had to leave hurriedly.

The *Sydney* caught her and badly damaged her. The *Emden* went aground and eventually surrendered.

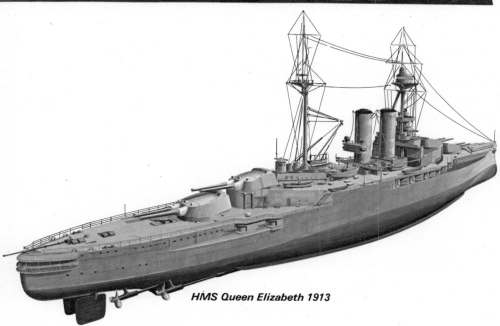

The British Super Dreadnought, HMS *Queen Elizabeth* (left), was launched in 1913. She was 31,000 tons and carried eight 15in and twelve 6in guns. This, and other modernized ships of her class also served in World War II.

HMS Queen Elizabeth 1913

Naval arms race

During the long years of relative world peace between the Napoleonic and 1914-18 wars, the navies of the world were in turmoil.

Nelson's fleet of wooden ships-of-the-line had been rendered obsolete by the advent of steam, the introduction of iron and steel, and rifled guns and explosive shells.

By the early 1900's hostility was growing as the newly-formed Germany challenged Britain's commercial position in the world. Outward signs of the new hostility was a naval arms race. The British Admiralty made a major advance in warship design when it ordered the *Dreadnought* in 1906. This ship was so different that she gave her name to all ships of her type. Based on lessons learned from the Russo-Japanese war, the *Dreadnought* carried more big, long-range guns, by completely eliminating the secondary armament which had proved so useless. In future, secondary armament was restricted to the short-range quick-firing gun for use against torpedo boats and later, aircraft.

Battle of the Dreadnoughts

The *Dreadnought* made all older battleships out-of-date. Germany speeded up her program and introduced Dreadnought-type ships. Britain, who depended on naval supremacy for the security of her Empire, followed suit. By the outbreak of war in 1914, Germany had 15 Dreadnoughts to Britain's 22.

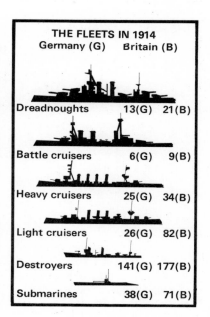

THE FLEETS IN 1914
Germany (G)   Britain (B)

	Germany (G)	Britain (B)
Dreadnoughts	13(G)	21(B)
Battle cruisers	6(G)	9(B)
Heavy cruisers	25(G)	34(B)
Light cruisers	26(G)	82(B)
Destroyers	141(G)	177(B)
Submarines	38(G)	71(B)

Early submarine warfare

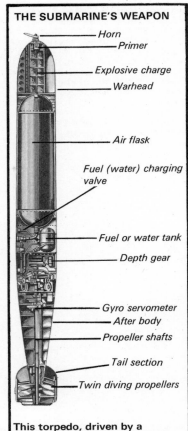

- Horn
- Primer
- Explosive charge
- Warhead
- Air flask
- Fuel (water) charging valve
- Fuel or water tank
- Depth gear
- Gyro servometer
- After body
- Propeller shafts
- Tail section
- Twin diving propellers

This torpedo, driven by a compressed air motor, carried 18lb of explosive several hundred yards at 30 knots.

These torpedoes could be fired either from the deck of a ship, or from under the water, which made them the ideal weapon for early submarines.

In 1915 the German Admiralty announced that its U-boats (*Unterseebooten*) would sink enemy ships without warning in the waters surrounding Great Britain and Ireland.

The standard forms of attack were either submerged by torpedo, or on the surface with gunfire.

Surface attacks gave the crew and passengers of the ship under fire warning to abandon ship. This warning was very important if neutral passengers were on board. World opinion, particularly in the United States, condemned attack without warning.

Germany ignored this disapproval, and pursued her underwater attacks. In two and a half months, and with only 20 submarines, Germany had sunk nearly 100 ships.

While Germany built more U-boats, the Royal Navy searched for an answer to the U-boat menace.

One answer was called the Q ship. These were secretly-armed merchant ships. They tempted U-boats to attack on the surface, and then revealed their own armament to fight back. A submarine on the surface was very vulnerable to gunfire.

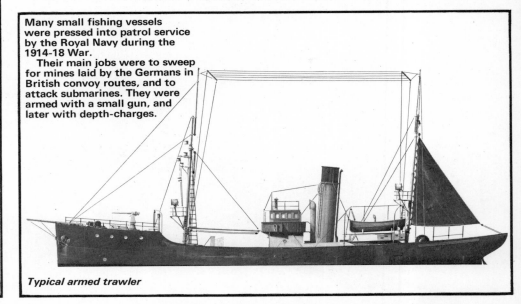

Many small fishing vessels were pressed into patrol service by the Royal Navy during the 1914-18 War.

Their main jobs were to sweep for mines laid by the Germans in British convoy routes, and to attack submarines. They were armed with a small gun, and later with depth-charges.

Typical armed trawler

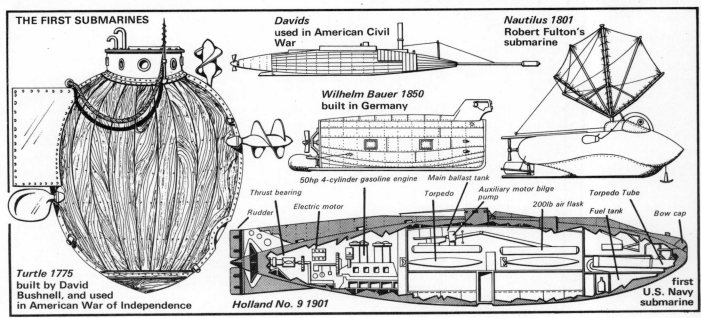

THE FIRST SUBMARINES

Davids used in American Civil War

Nautilus 1801 Robert Fulton's submarine

Wilhelm Bauer 1850 built in Germany

50hp 4-cylinder gasoline engine — Main ballast tank — Auxiliary motor bilge pump — Torpedo Tube

Thrust bearing — Torpedo — 200lb air flask — Fuel tank — Bow cap

Rudder — Electric motor

Turtle 1775 built by David Bushnell, and used in American War of Independence

Holland No. 9 1901

first U.S. Navy submarine

The depth-charge

The main defenses against U-boats at this time were destroyers, torpedo boats, armed trawlers and yachts. All proved almost useless except to force the U-boats to submerge until they had passed. It wasn't until the depth-charge was introduced, in 1916, that warships began to sink the subs in any numbers.

In 1917 the convoy system, so well-known in previous centuries, was re-introduced. Large groups of merchant-men were escorted through dangerous waters by warships. Losses were reduced considerably, and more U-boats were sunk, as now they could only attack ships in the presence of sloops or destroyers carrying depth-charges.

This U9 submarine (below), though not typical of later U-boats, played an important part in the development of submarine warfare in Germany. It showed the German Admiralty what U-boats could do. In September 1914 the U9, already small and out-of-date, attacked and sank three British cruisers. This success, together with the failures of the German surface raiders after the end of 1914, persuaded the Germans to increase the U-boat strength.

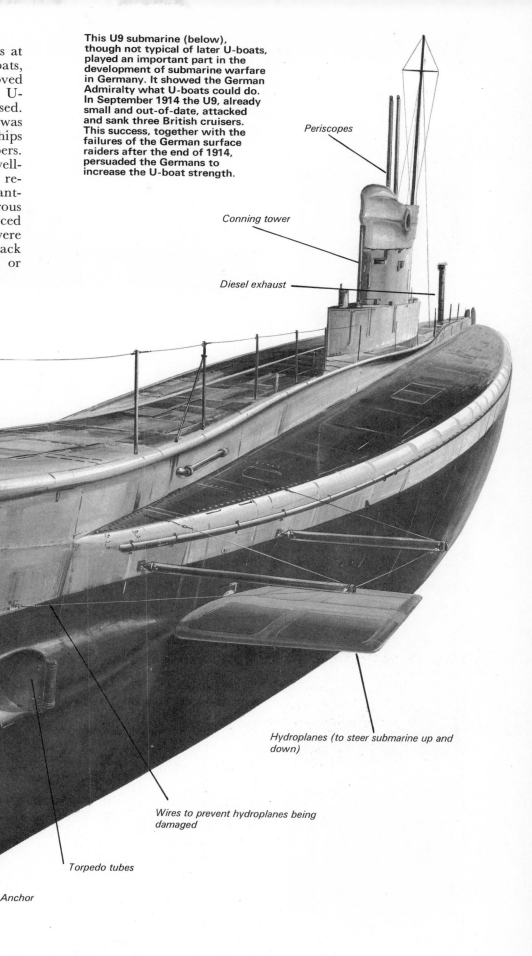

Periscopes

Conning tower

Diesel exhaust

Identification number

Hydroplanes (to steer submarine up and down)

Wires to prevent hydroplanes being damaged

Torpedo tubes

Anchor

U9 submarine

The Blue Riband Atlantic passenger liners

LUXURY AT SEA

First class passengers on the *Mauretania* dined as well on board as in the famous Paris restaurants.

The lounge rivaled those of luxury hotels on shore.

Tea was served in an elegant conservatory . . .

. . . and the cabins were elaborately furnished.

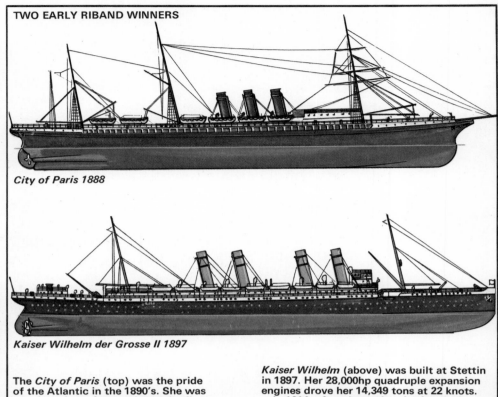

TWO EARLY RIBAND WINNERS

City of Paris 1888

Kaiser Wilhelm der Grosse II 1897

The *City of Paris* (top) was the pride of the Atlantic in the 1890's. She was very luxurious, fast, and was the first Atlantic liner to have two propellers. The steel-built *City of Paris* had a tonnage of 14,500 tons.

Kaiser Wilhelm (above) was built at Stettin in 1897. Her 28,000hp quadruple expansion engines drove her 14,349 tons at 22 knots.
In 1914, after the outbreak of war, she was converted into a raiding ship to attack British and French merchant ships. She was sunk shortly afterwards by HMS *Highflyer*.

National prestige

The romance of ships in the 20th century has been closely tied to the great Atlantic liners. The battle for the Blue Riband, awarded for the fastest Atlantic crossing, has involved the national prestige of the countries whose ships competed for it across the Atlantic.

The rewards for the holder were large. The transatlantic route was the busiest and richest route in the world in the days before high-speed jet aircraft became the commonest way of traveling between America and Europe. The newest, or fastest, or largest of the many liners was sure to be full of the wealthy and famous.

To satisfy the needs of these passengers, the steamers became more like vast floating hotels, with ballrooms, menus to rival those of the best hotels in the world, and a social life to ensure that the rich need never realize that they had been at sea.

The first Atlantic liner

The history of liners started in 1838 when the *Great Western* started a packet delivery service, followed in 1840 by the first regular Cunard crossing. This started with the *Britannia*.

The first major change in Atlantic liners, apart from a steady increase in size, was the introduction of steam turbines, in the *Mauretania* and *Lusitania* built in 1907 for Cunard. The *Mauretania*, the faster of the two, had a trial speed of over 27 knots, and a gross tonnage of 31,938. Turbine power now became standard for liners, but the *Mauretania* held the Blue Riband until 1929.

Germany, France, and Britain then held the Riband in quick succession until America gained it in 1952, with the *United States*. She was the last great liner built solely for the Atlantic run, as Britain's *Queen Elizabeth 2* was designed more as a floating holiday resort, spending half her time cruising.

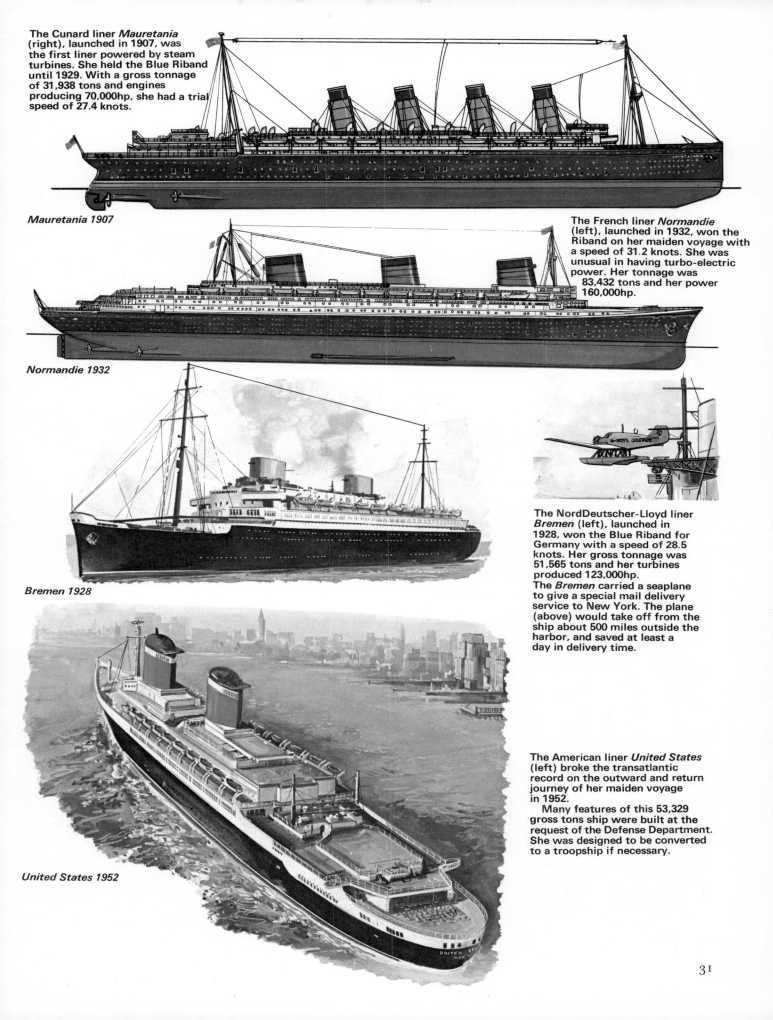

The Cunard liner *Mauretania* (right), launched in 1907, was the first liner powered by steam turbines. She held the Blue Riband until 1929. With a gross tonnage of 31,938 tons and engines producing 70,000hp, she had a trial speed of 27.4 knots.

Mauretania 1907

The French liner *Normandie* (left), launched in 1932, won the Riband on her maiden voyage with a speed of 31.2 knots. She was unusual in having turbo-electric power. Her tonnage was 83,432 tons and her power 160,000hp.

Normandie 1932

Bremen 1928

The NordDeutscher-Lloyd liner *Bremen* (left), launched in 1928, won the Blue Riband for Germany with a speed of 28.5 knots. Her gross tonnage was 51,565 tons and her turbines produced 123,000hp.
The *Bremen* carried a seaplane to give a special mail delivery service to New York. The plane (above) would take off from the ship about 500 miles outside the harbor, and saved at least a day in delivery time.

The American liner *United States* (left) broke the transatlantic record on the outward and return journey of her maiden voyage in 1952.
Many features of this 53,329 gross tons ship were built at the request of the Defense Department. She was designed to be converted to a troopship if necessary.

United States 1952

31

World War II battle of the Atlantic

Germany's type 1X-92 U-boat was designed for high surface speed and heavy armament. At 1,606 to 1,804 tons it had a surface speed of 19¼ knots and 7 knots submerged; with a range of 23,700 miles, but a range of only 57 miles submerged, and that at a speed of only 4 knots. It carried 24 torpedoes for 6 tubes.

Type VII-B played a leading role in the early part of the Battle of the Atlantic, although in 1939 there were only 18 of this type. At 753 to 857 tons this U-boat had a surface speed of 17¼ knots and 8 knots submerged. Its range was 6,500 miles, 80 miles submerged, and carried 12 torpedoes for five tubes.

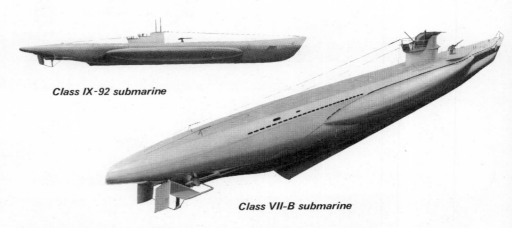

Class IX-92 submarine

Class VII-B submarine

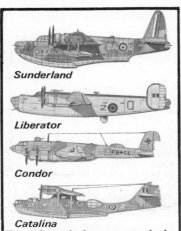

Sunderland

Liberator

Condor

Catalina

These four airplanes are typical of the Allied shore-based aircraft which was closely involved in the battle against the U-boat. The Germans also used shore-based aircraft to scout for the U-boats.

The fight against the U-boats

The battle against the U-boats in World War II just carried on where it had left off in 1918. The British started the convoy system again, but did not have enough escort ships. The Germans did not have enough U-boats to take full advantage of this weakness.

Both sides were building new vessels as fast as they could, because whichever side got a definite advantage would finally win the battle.

Air power tried for the first time to influence a naval battle. On one side aircraft would find and attack U-boats, on the other they would find convoys and guide U-boats to the attack. The air forces also bombed the enemy's shipyards and ports.

The German U-boats, however, were slowly winning through.

New weapons

In 1942 America and Britain were losing about 100 ships a month, while the U-boat fleet was increasing by 12 boats a month. Then new and improved methods of detecting submarines were discovered. More efficient weapons were introduced. More long-range aircraft also became available.

Two new weapons in particular finally turned the tide. The first was the escort carrier, a small aircraft carrier for escorting convoys on the Atlantic. Their aircraft meant that a submarine was never safe on the surface. The other weapon was the support groups. These were made up from a group of spare escort ships which were free to go to the aid of any convoy under threat of attack. From this time ship losses decreased and U-boat losses increased.

EMERGENCY SHIPBUILDING

One of the main weapons in the Battle of the Atlantic was not really a weapon in the true sense, but its contribution to the Allied victory was immense. These simple *Liberty* cargo ships could be built in parts by people not used to shipbuilding. This enabled the Allies to more than replace their war losses, and to build more warships. Many are still in use today.

Typical convoy pattern

This diagram of a convoy shows how merchant ships were protected by flying boats and warships. (Distances between ships are not to scale.)

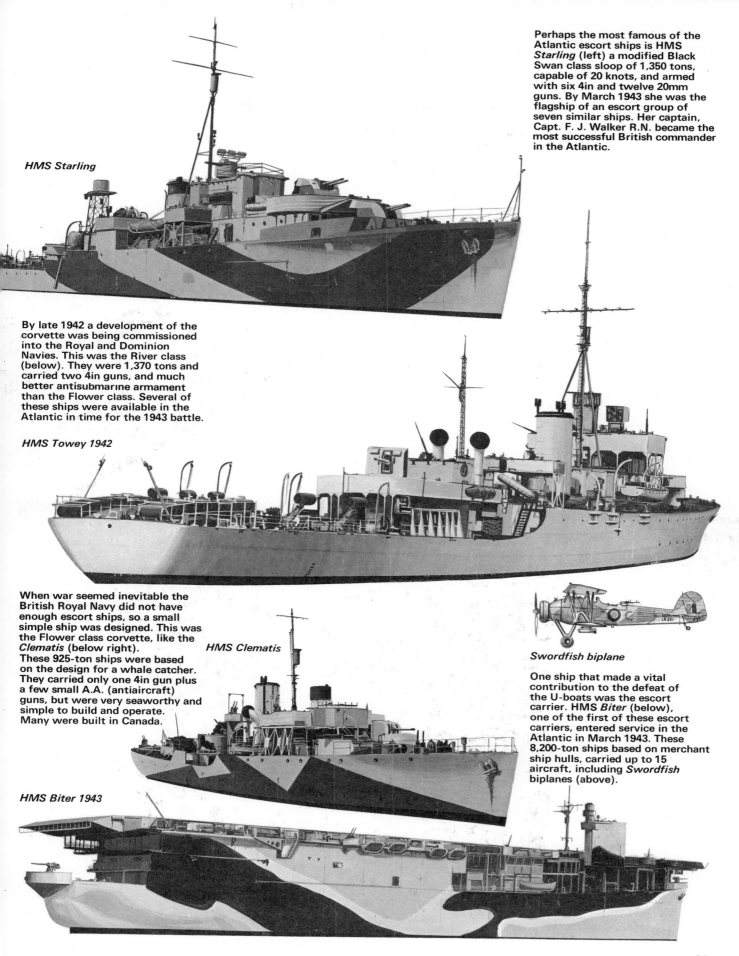

HMS Starling

Perhaps the most famous of the Atlantic escort ships is HMS *Starling* (left) a modified Black Swan class sloop of 1,350 tons, capable of 20 knots, and armed with six 4in and twelve 20mm guns. By March 1943 she was the flagship of an escort group of seven similar ships. Her captain, Capt. F. J. Walker R.N. became the most successful British commander in the Atlantic.

By late 1942 a development of the corvette was being commissioned into the Royal and Dominion Navies. This was the River class (below). They were 1,370 tons and carried two 4in guns, and much better antisubmarine armament than the Flower class. Several of these ships were available in the Atlantic in time for the 1943 battle.

HMS Towey 1942

When war seemed inevitable the British Royal Navy did not have enough escort ships, so a small simple ship was designed. This was the Flower class corvette, like the *Clematis* (below right). These 925-ton ships were based on the design for a whale catcher. They carried only one 4in gun plus a few small A.A. (antiaircraft) guns, but were very seaworthy and simple to build and operate. Many were built in Canada.

HMS Clematis

Swordfish biplane

One ship that made a vital contribution to the defeat of the U-boats was the escort carrier. HMS *Biter* (below), one of the first of these escort carriers, entered service in the Atlantic in March 1943. These 8,200-ton ships based on merchant ship hulls, carried up to 15 aircraft, including *Swordfish* biplanes (above).

HMS Biter 1943

Aircraft carriers the war in the Pacific

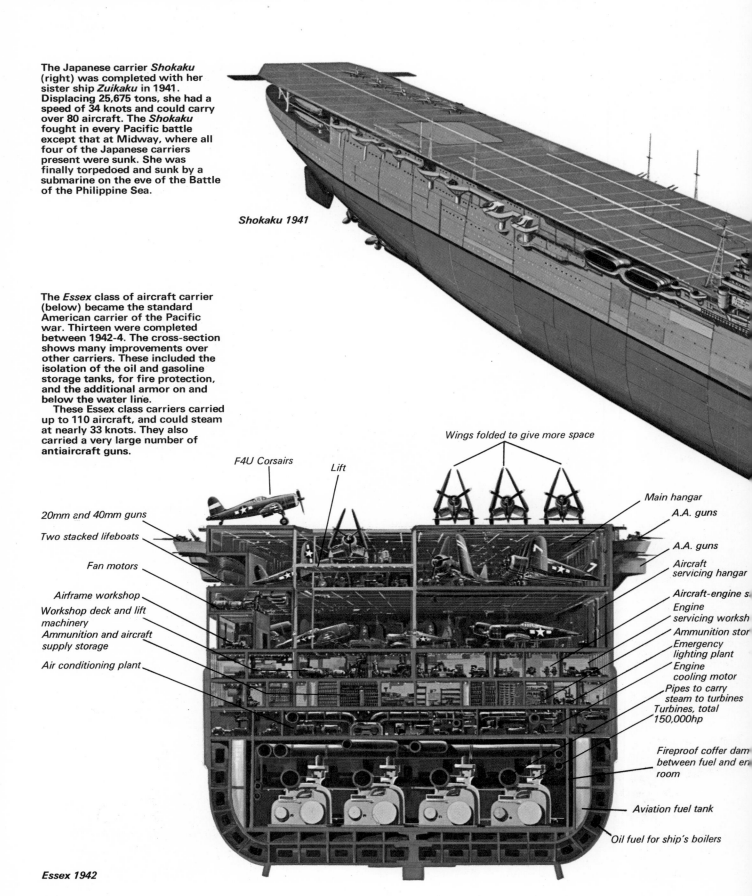

The Japanese carrier *Shokaku* (right) was completed with her sister ship *Zuikaku* in 1941. Displacing 25,675 tons, she had a speed of 34 knots and could carry over 80 aircraft. The *Shokaku* fought in every Pacific battle except that at Midway, where all four of the Japanese carriers present were sunk. She was finally torpedoed and sunk by a submarine on the eve of the Battle of the Philippine Sea.

Shokaku 1941

The *Essex* class of aircraft carrier (below) became the standard American carrier of the Pacific war. Thirteen were completed between 1942-4. The cross-section shows many improvements over other carriers. These included the isolation of the oil and gasoline storage tanks, for fire protection, and the additional armor on and below the water line.

These Essex class carriers carried up to 110 aircraft, and could steam at nearly 33 knots. They also carried a very large number of antiaircraft guns.

F4U Corsairs

Lift

Wings folded to give more space

20mm and 40mm guns

Two stacked lifeboats

Fan motors

Airframe workshop

Workshop deck and lift machinery

Ammunition and aircraft supply storage

Air conditioning plant

Main hangar

A.A. guns

A.A. guns

Aircraft servicing hangar

Aircraft-engine s...

Engine servicing worksh...

Ammunition stor...

Emergency lighting plant

Engine cooling motor

Pipes to carry steam to turbines

Turbines, total 150,000hp

Fireproof coffer dam between fuel and en... room

Aviation fuel tank

Oil fuel for ship's boilers

Essex 1942

Pearl Harbor

The Atlantic war was in many ways just a continuation of the U-boat battle of the 1914-18 war, but the Pacific war was an entirely new type of war. It started when 350 Japanese aircraft took off from six carriers to attack the American fleet in Pearl Harbor. This attack, which almost wiped out the American fleet, set the pattern in the Pacific. The naval war was to be fought between unseen fleets, launching massive air attacks.

The Japanese followed up this success by sinking two British battleships with shore-based naval aircraft. They finally proved that sea power now depended more upon naval aircraft than on big guns.

Japan loses ground

Carrier battles raged across the Pacific as these floating airdromes sought to destroy each other.

The scale of these battles can be judged from the sizes of the fleets. The first battle was at Coral Sea, where Japan's invasion attempt against New Guinea was halted. Japan had three carriers with 147 aircraft, and the US two carriers with 163 aircraft. Two years later the roles were reversed. A Japanese force with nine carriers and 450 aircraft tried to prevent an American landing in the Philippine Sea supported by fifteen carriers with 906 aircraft.

THE CARRIER'S WEAPON

Japanese A6M Zero

This famous Japanese fighter fought right through the war. It was capable of 351mph.

USN Wildcat

The American answer to the *Zero* from 1943 onwards had a maximum speed of 376mph.

Japanese B5N Kate

The *Kate* was very similar to the *Dauntless,* but carried 1,500lb and reached 264mph.

USN SBD Dauntless

This dive-bomber could carry a bomb of up to 1,000lb and reached a maximum speed of 250mph.

The Allied submarine campaign against the Japanese merchant ships was very effective. By August 1945, her merchant fleet was only one eighth of its original size, and five ships were being sunk for every new one built. Allied submarines also sank eight carriers and many other warships. Typical was this American T-class submarine of 1,475 to 2,370 tons (below), capable of 20 knots on the surface and 8.7 knots submerged.

USN T class submarine

35

New ships for new jobs

A large part of the cost of shipping freight is the cost of loading and unloading in port. There is also the cost of paying and feeding a ship's crew while in harbor.

The container ship (right) reduces loading time and effort, and is therefore more economical. Containers, really only very large boxes of standard sizes, can be filled at the factory and then carried on the back of a flat truck and lifted by crane straight into a special nest on a ship.

Container ship

OIL RIG

Oil rigs carry equipment and a crew of 40 to 60 men to drill for oil below the sea bed.

A special class of ship for servicing the rigs has developed. Helicopters and small boats are also used for delivering supplies and changing the crews.

When the steel rigs are working, they sit on legs resting on the sea bed. The legs can be pulled up so that the rig can be towed to another site.

One of the largest oil tankers in the world (right) carries over 300,000 tons of oil from the Persian Gulf to oil refineries in Europe.

The *Universe Ireland* is over 1,000ft long and 175ft wide. (Compare her with the coastal tanker *Esso Tynemouth* shown alongside in white.) She is powered by two steam turbines totaling 37,400hp. She travels at 14 knots.

Changes in world trade

Since World War II, the pattern of world trade has altered. Britain ceased to be the largest maritime nation. Countries with favorable tax and wage laws, like Panama and Liberia, took over the lead (although the ships registered in these countries are not necessarily owned there). The large numbers of surplus Liberty ships bought cheaply after the war as an investment, helped this to come about.

Europe ceased to be the so-called workshop absorbing the supplies of raw materials from the rest of the world. The underdeveloped nations were all striving to establish themselves as industrial powers and began to challenge Europe's position.

The passenger liners have been challenged by air travel, and the liner companies have had to devise new ships and new routes to meet this challenge.

New cargoes

Oil has become the most important cargo. Since the closing of the Suez Canal, giant tankers have been built which are too large for the canal but which can carry oil from the Persian Gulf around Africa more cheaply than the smaller ones using the Suez.

Better ways of handling cargo have been developed, which cut the time a ship spends in harbor from days to hours. Finally, the tremendous growth of trade and tourism in Europe has led to the development of car and truck ferries which cross the short sea routes.

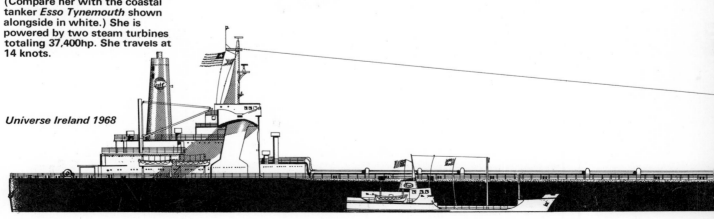

Universe Ireland 1968

36

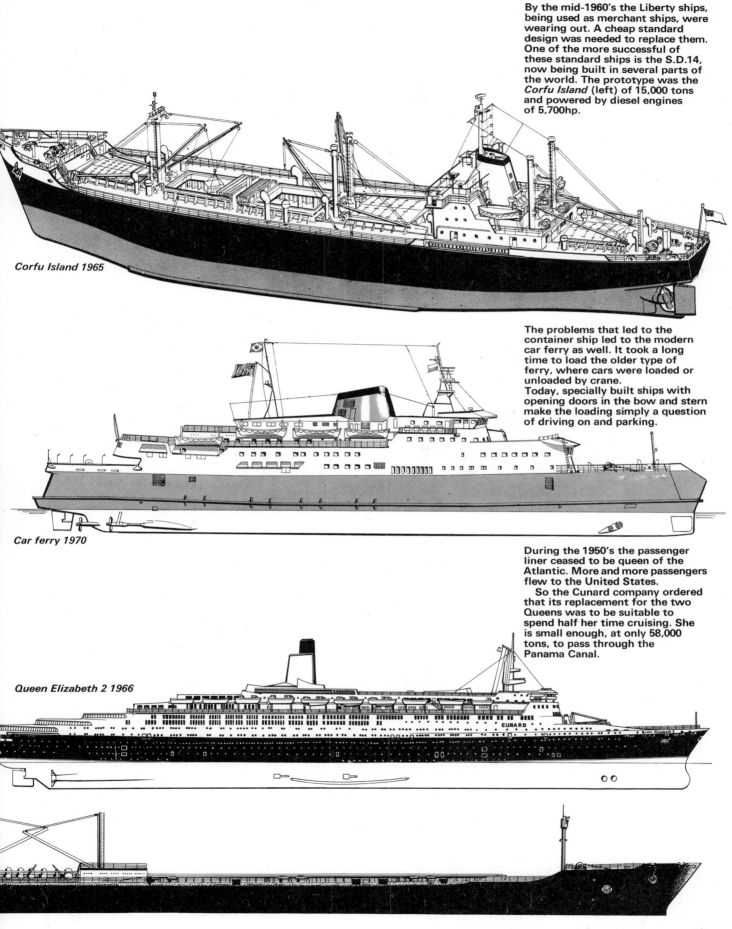

By the mid-1960's the Liberty ships, being used as merchant ships, were wearing out. A cheap standard design was needed to replace them. One of the more successful of these standard ships is the S.D.14, now being built in several parts of the world. The prototype was the *Corfu Island* (left) of 15,000 tons and powered by diesel engines of 5,700hp.

Corfu Island 1965

The problems that led to the container ship led to the modern car ferry as well. It took a long time to load the older type of ferry, where cars were loaded or unloaded by crane.
Today, specially built ships with opening doors in the bow and stern make the loading simply a question of driving on and parking.

Car ferry 1970

During the 1950's the passenger liner ceased to be queen of the Atlantic. More and more passengers flew to the United States.
So the Cunard company ordered that its replacement for the two Queens was to be suitable to spend half her time cruising. She is small enough, at only 58,000 tons, to pass through the Panama Canal.

Queen Elizabeth 2 1966

Boating for pleasure and sport

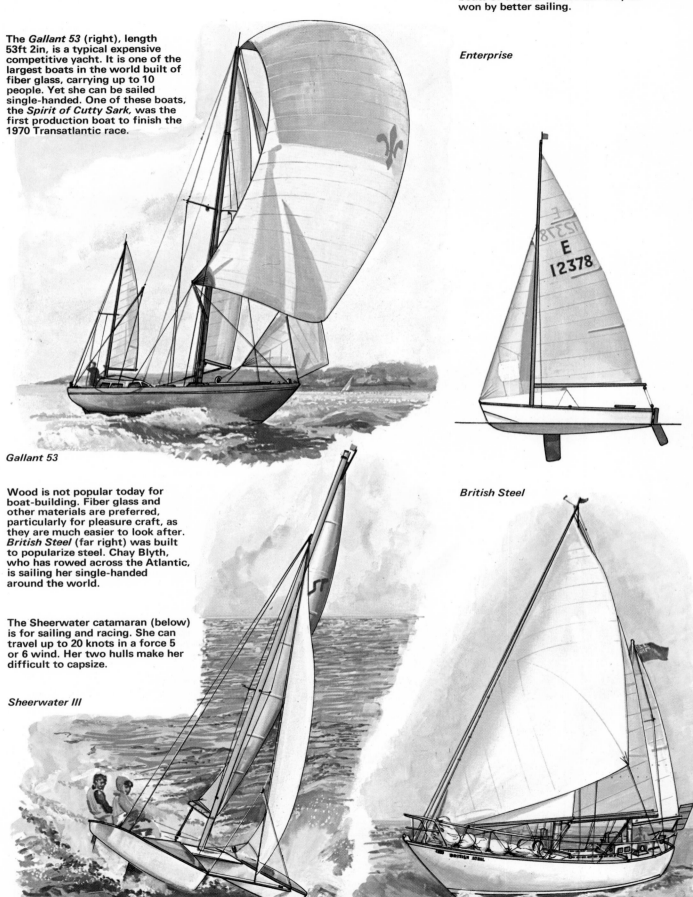

The *Enterprise* (below) is typical of the hundreds of thousands of small sailing dinghies. It is built to controlled specifications, and races between several boats of the same class can only be won by better sailing.

The *Gallant 53* (right), length 53ft 2in, is a typical expensive competitive yacht. It is one of the largest boats in the world built of fiber glass, carrying up to 10 people. Yet she can be sailed single-handed. One of these boats, the *Spirit of Cutty Sark,* was the first production boat to finish the 1970 Transatlantic race.

Enterprise

Gallant 53

E 12378

Wood is not popular today for boat-building. Fiber glass and other materials are preferred, particularly for pleasure craft, as they are much easier to look after. *British Steel* (far right) was built to popularize steel. Chay Blyth, who has rowed across the Atlantic, is sailing her single-handed around the world.

British Steel

The Sheerwater catamaran (below) is for sailing and racing. She can travel up to 20 knots in a force 5 or 6 wind. Her two hulls make her difficult to capsize.

Sheerwater III

Magnum Tornado

A very expensive, but very exciting water sport is that of power boat racing on the sea. Boats like the *Magnum Tornado* (left) can reach speeds of nearly 70mph, but it is not always the fastest boat that wins. The courses are over 150 miles long, and if the race is in rough weather, a slower, more seaworthy boat can win.

Fishing boat

For fishermen, a boat is only a platform to fish from, and a taxi to get out to the fishing grounds. The rather special type (left) is used to fish for big game fish, like sharks.

Water skiing boat

While the boat shown above may look like the racer (top), it is much smaller and cheaper. It is powered by an outboard motor of about 60hp and is used to tow water skiers.

Hi-Foil 2

This little boat is only 9ft long, but it can carry two people at a top speed of 35mph because it is powered by a hydrofoil.

Specialized and experimental ships

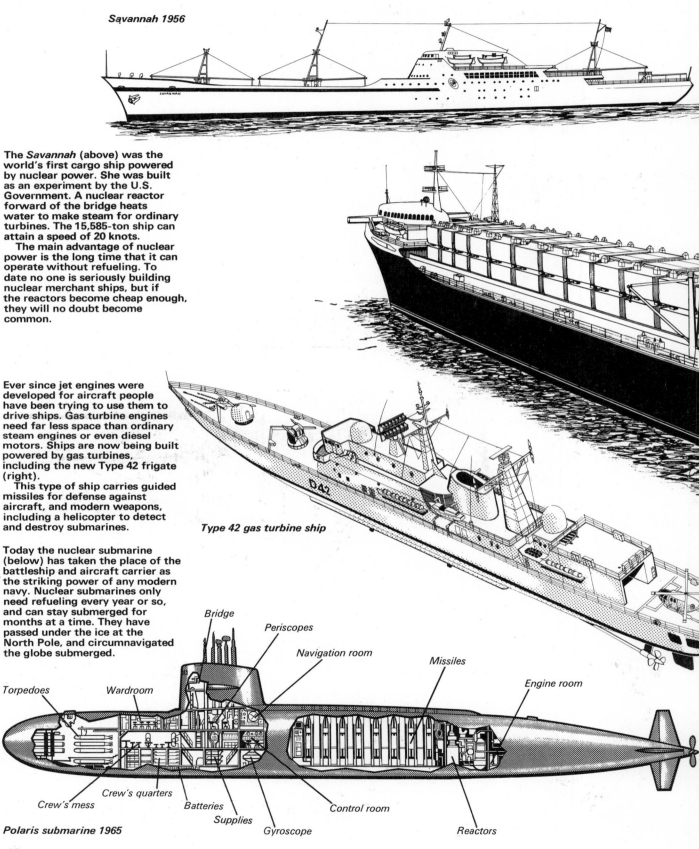

Savannah 1956

The *Savannah* (above) was the world's first cargo ship powered by nuclear power. She was built as an experiment by the U.S. Government. A nuclear reactor forward of the bridge heats water to make steam for ordinary turbines. The 15,585-ton ship can attain a speed of 20 knots.

The main advantage of nuclear power is the long time that it can operate without refueling. To date no one is seriously building nuclear merchant ships, but if the reactors become cheap enough, they will no doubt become common.

Ever since jet engines were developed for aircraft people have been trying to use them to drive ships. Gas turbine engines need far less space than ordinary steam engines or even diesel motors. Ships are now being built powered by gas turbines, including the new Type 42 frigate (right).

This type of ship carries guided missiles for defense against aircraft, and modern weapons, including a helicopter to detect and destroy submarines.

Type 42 gas turbine ship

Today the nuclear submarine (below) has taken the place of the battleship and aircraft carrier as the striking power of any modern navy. Nuclear submarines only need refueling every year or so, and can stay submerged for months at a time. They have passed under the ice at the North Pole, and circumnavigated the globe submerged.

Bridge

Periscopes

Navigation room

Missiles

Engine room

Torpedoes

Wardroom

Crew's quarters

Crew's mess

Batteries

Supplies

Gyroscope

Control room

Reactors

Polaris submarine 1965

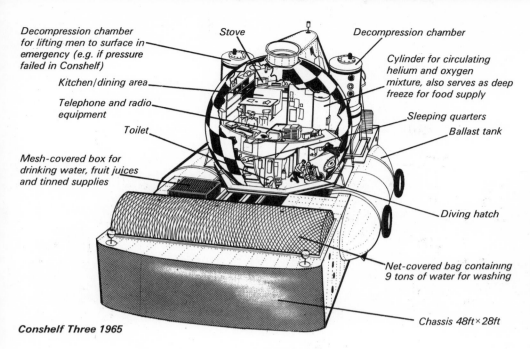

Decompression chamber for lifting men to surface in emergency (e.g. if pressure failed in Conshelf)

Stove

Decompression chamber

Kitchen/dining area

Cylinder for circulating helium and oxygen mixture, also serves as deep freeze for food supply

Telephone and radio equipment

Sleeping quarters

Toilet

Ballast tank

Mesh-covered box for drinking water, fruit juices and tinned supplies

Diving hatch

Net-covered bag containing 9 tons of water for washing

Chassis 48ft × 28ft

Conshelf Three 1965

In September 1965 a crew of six oceanauts spent three weeks on the floor of the Mediterranean in *Conshelf* (Continental Shelf Station) *Three* (left). It sat on adjustable legs at a depth of 328 ft. Captain Jacques-Yves Cousteau directed the project from the surface.

The first manned undersea base was established in 1962. This third experiment was concerned with finding out whether plant life could survive under artificial light on the dark sea bottom.

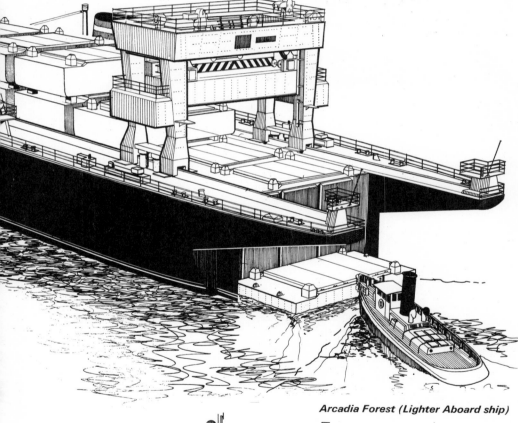

Many ports do not yet have cranes and wharves which can take the large containers. This has led to the development of a new type of vessel (left) which, instead of carrying containers, carries its own fleet of lighters, or barges. It operates in the same way as a container ship, by pre-loading the barges while the ship is at sea. When she gets to port the barges are exchanged for ones pre-loaded at the port.

These vessels are sometimes referred to as LASH, or Lighter Aboard ships.

Arcadia Forest (Lighter Aboard ship)

Lenin 1960

The 25,000-ton Russian ice breaker *Lenin* (left) is nuclear powered. It is used in the Baltic, where Russian ports are frozen for much of the year. The ice breaker keeps the ports open for trade. Similar ships are being used in Canada, and will become increasingly important in Alaska, where new oil fields are being established.

Surface skimmers

A large hovercraft, the *SRN4* (right), is challenging the car ferries connecting Britain with France. It is large enough to carry 30 cars and up to 250 passengers at speeds up to 70 knots. It travels on a cushion of air, and is powered by four large jet engines of the type used to power large airliners. It is driven by large aircraft-type propellers. The air cushion is kept in place by tough rubber 'skirts' which hang down all around.

SRN4 hovercraft

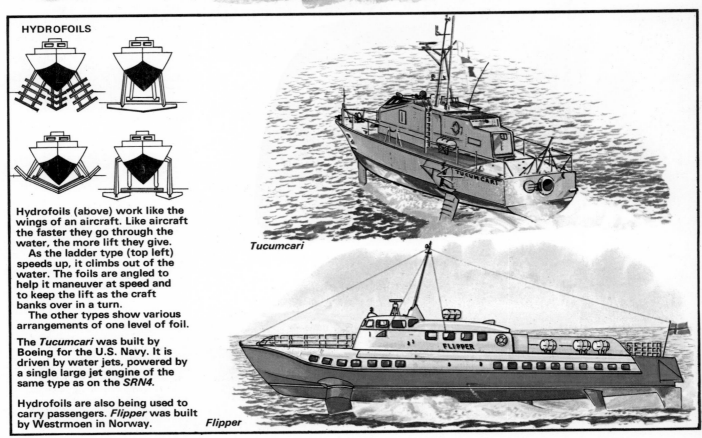

HYDROFOILS

Hydrofoils (above) work like the wings of an aircraft. Like aircraft the faster they go through the water, the more lift they give.

As the ladder type (top left) speeds up, it climbs out of the water. The foils are angled to help it maneuver at speed and to keep the lift as the craft banks over in a turn.

The other types show various arrangements of one level of foil.

The *Tucumcari* was built by Boeing for the U.S. Navy. It is driven by water jets, powered by a single large jet engine of the same type as on the *SRN4*.

Hydrofoils are also being used to carry passengers. *Flipper* was built by Westrmoen in Norway.

Tucumcari

Flipper

Projects

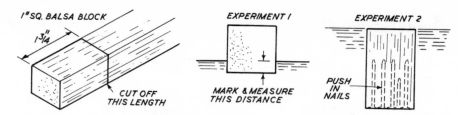

Buoyancy and stability

For any solid material to float it must be lighter than water. A cubic foot of water weighs $62\frac{1}{4}$lbs, therefore $1\frac{3}{4}$cu in of water weighs almost 1oz.

Cut off a $1\frac{3}{4}$in length of 1in sq balsa block. This will weigh less than 1oz, so it will float (*Experiment 1*). The submerged part of the block will *displace* or take the place of an equal amount of water.

For *Experiment 2*, make the block heavier with 1in wire nails. Add nails until the block is on the point of sinking. This time the block is displacing an amount of water equal to the full volume of the block.

Calculations: If we multiply 1oz by the depth to which the block submerges we have the *weight* of the block in ounces. Thus if the block submerges to a depth of $\frac{1}{5}$in its weight is $\frac{1}{5}$th of an ounce. You can work out the weight of other wood blocks in a similar way, provided they are all $1\frac{3}{4}$in long by 1in sq.

In *Experiment 2* the block is displacing a full $1\frac{3}{4}$cu in of water, which should weigh 1oz. Dry the block and check that it does. Now work out the weight of water in pounds per cubic feet. Multiply the weight of the block *in ounces* by 108 and divide by the volume of the block in cubic inches ($1\frac{3}{4}$ or $\frac{7}{4}$). See if this works out to $62\frac{1}{4}$. This works for any size of block.

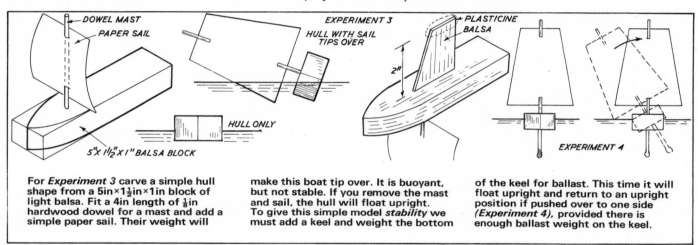

For *Experiment 3* carve a simple hull shape from a 5in×1½in×1in block of light balsa. Fit a 4in length of $\frac{1}{8}$in hardwood dowel for a mast and add a simple paper sail. Their weight will make this boat tip over. It is buoyant, but not stable. If you remove the mast and sail, the hull will float upright. To give this simple model *stability* we must add a keel and weight the bottom of the keel for ballast. This time it will float upright and return to an upright position if pushed over to one side (*Experiment 4*), provided there is enough ballast weight on the keel.

Carrying extra weight

Remove the mast and sail from the model used in *Experiment 4* and float it in water. Add coins or metal washers carefully one at a time until the top of the hull is level with the surface of the water (*Experiment 5*). Weigh the coins.

Now hollow out the hull until the sides and bottom are as thin as you can get them. Add weights along the center of the hull (*Experiment 6*). This time the hull will be much more stable, because the weight is being placed lower down in the hull. It will also carry a little more weight, because hollowing out has reduced the weight of the hull.

Finally, make up a much lighter hull of the same size from $\frac{1}{16}$in sheet balsa. See how much more this light hull will carry (*Experiment 7*) than the other two. And since all the weight can be placed low down in the hull it will be stable enough without a keel. Only sailing ships need keels. Other types of ships can be made stable by placing weight, or *ballast*, low down in the hull.

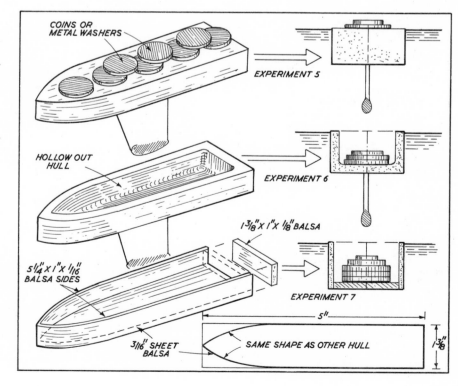

Projects sailing boats and hovercraft

Evolution of the ship

A simple model will show that a log 'boat' (1) floated, but it was not stable. The dug-out canoe (2) was not much better, although it could carry more weight with slightly better stability.

The raft (3) was a much better idea. This has good carrying ability and it is almost impossible to tip over.

The next step was to fit a log raft with a mast and sail, like the model shown (4). If you add a steering oar, or rudder, it will keep a straight course across a pond.

The next step was to try to make boats faster and easier to handle. This meant going back to a canoe-shaped hull capable of cutting its way through the water. A clever idea was to join two canoe-shaped hulls with a center piece to give the same width and stability as a raft, but with far less resistance to being driven through the water. Try out the *catamaran* (5). Try it out against the raft (4) and see how much faster it sails. The *trimaran* (6) is another variation.

Much later, sailing ships got bigger, broader, and deeper, in order to carry more weight. They also became very top heavy (7) and were often in danger of turning over. So sailing ship hulls were made longer, lower and more slender. They got their stability from ballast weight placed low down in the hull. All *model* sailing ships, however, need a keel to sail properly.

Try building different models. You should find that the longer the hull (8) the faster it can be made to sail.

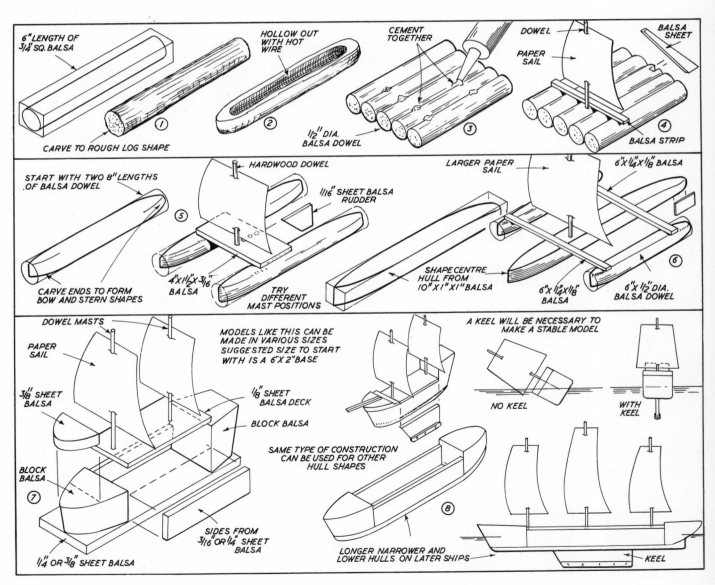

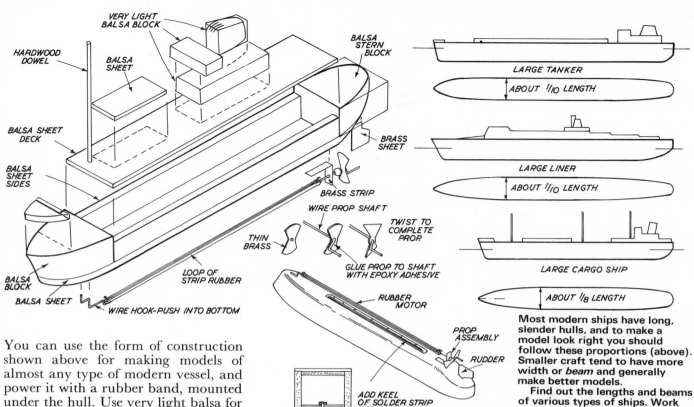

You can use the form of construction shown above for making models of almost any type of modern vessel, and power it with a rubber band, mounted under the hull. Use very light balsa for the superstructure parts, otherwise you will need a lot of keel weight for stability.

Hovercraft

This model hovercraft demonstrates the air cushion principle, and will operate over any really smooth surface.

For the fan, cut a $2\frac{3}{4}$in diameter circle from thin aluminium sheet, with further cuts for the blades (A). Cut two hub pieces from sheet balsa and glue in place with epoxy adhesive (B). Now bend each fan blade to shape (C).

Build a frame, using 1in $\times \frac{1}{16}$in balsa (D). Note how the sides are angled towards the top at each end. Cut and fit the top (E).

For power, you need a small electric motor. Bore a hole in the fan hub and press on to the motor shaft. Mount the motor in the hole in the top, using $\frac{1}{2}$in $\times \frac{3}{3.2}$in balsa (two main drawings). The simple battery box cements on to these strips, to hold the bottom of the motor in place.

Check that the fan spins evenly when the motor is connected to the battery. Then make a funnel from stiff paper to surround the upper part of the motor and fan, cementing this into the top cut-out. Drill two small holes in one end of the base. Air escaping through these holes will provide sufficient 'jet' thrust to propel the hovercraft forward over a level surface.

Most modern ships have long, slender hulls, and to make a model look right you should follow these proportions (above). Smaller craft tend to have more width or *beam* and generally make better models.

Find out the lengths and beams of various types of ships. Work out the length-to-beam ratio (length divided by the beam).

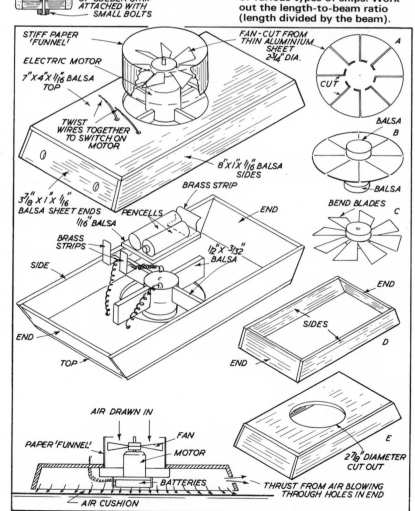

Projects submarines

This model demonstrates the 'working principle' of a submarine.

The power unit is a rubber band, driving a simple propeller at the stern. The rubber motor is housed inside the hull, the front end being taken out through a hole drilled in the deck and held in place with a cork pushed into this hole. The propeller assembly pulls out of the stern, so that you can 'fish' for the other end of the motor with a piece of bent wire to couple it up.

A hole in the bottom of the hull, sealed by another cork, is the 'flooding' control.

When flooded, and 'trimmed for diving' by adjusting the hydrovane, the pressure of water acting on the hydrovanes will force the bow down as the model is driven forward by the propeller. This will make the model run submerged, or with the top of the fin just showing. Experiment with different hydrovane settings to achieve the best results.

For surface running, 'pump out' the water ballast by removing the bottom cork and allowing it to drain. Then replace the cork. The model will now run with enough buoyancy to prevent the hydrovanes from forcing the bow into a dive: but to be correct the hydrovanes should be adjusted to a horizontal position for the best trim.

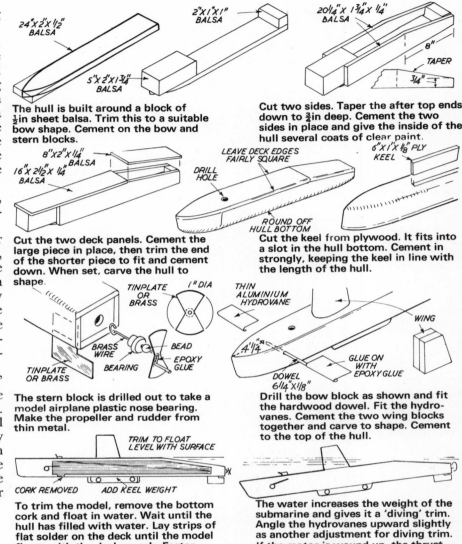

The hull is built around a block of ½in sheet balsa. Trim this to a suitable bow shape. Cement on the bow and stern blocks.

Cut two sides. Taper the after top ends down to ⅜in deep. Cement the two sides in place and give the inside of the hull several coats of clear paint.

Cut the two deck panels. Cement the large piece in place, then trim the end of the shorter piece to fit and cement down. When set, carve the hull to shape.

Cut the keel from plywood. It fits into a slot in the hull bottom. Cement in strongly, keeping the keel in line with the length of the hull.

The stern block is drilled out to take a model airplane plastic nose bearing. Make the propeller and rudder from thin metal.

Drill the bow block as shown and fit the hardwood dowel. Fit the hydrovanes. Cement the two wing blocks together and carve to shape. Cement to the top of the hull.

To trim the model, remove the bottom cork and float in water. Wait until the hull has filled with water. Lay strips of flat solder on the deck until the model floats with the deck awash. Fasten these solder strips on each side of the keel piece, to form ballast weights.

The water increases the weight of the submarine and gives it a 'diving' trim. Angle the hydrovanes upward slightly as another adjustment for diving trim. If the motor is wound up, the thrust from the propeller will drive the model forward into a dive.

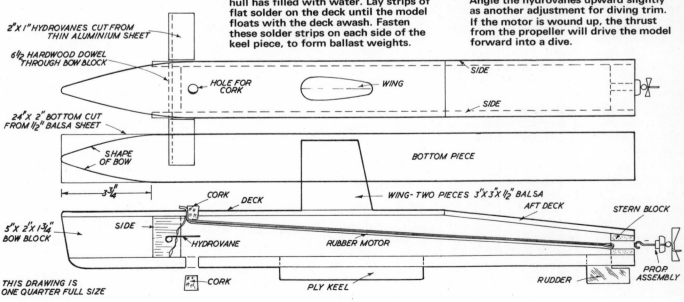

THIS DRAWING IS ONE QUARTER FULL SIZE

Index